A Boy Arrives

by
Stephen Meek

The man smiled again, uncertain how to proceed. He looked around, as though expecting to see the guardian angel of ticket checkers standing behind him with his wings open and a word of friendly advice on his lips. Seeing no-one, he looked back at Grimwood, his eyes searching for clues. Surely this rather untidy, bemused looking gentleman couldn't be the owner of Dunnydark?

A Boy Arrives is a tale full of gentle humour and affection, long-listed in The Times/Chicken House Competition for Best Children's Book.

I wouldn't be at all surprised to see it on our television screens before too long.
The School Librarian, Autumn 2012

One of the funniest books I've ever read!
William Shirras, critic, aged 11

For capable readers who like to laugh.

A Boy Arrives

Text copyright©2012 Stephen Meek
Cover©2012 Sally Townsend
All rights reserved
ISBN 978-1-908577-33-7

The rights of the author have been asserted

Conditions of Sale

British Library Cataloguing in Publication Data.
A catalogue record for this book is available from the
British Library.

First Edition

Hawkwood Books 2012

To
Pat and Bill

Chapter 1

Grimwood Streep had never experienced anything supernatural in his life, until one day, whilst in his library looking for a book on garden birds, he heard the sound of an angel singing.

'My word,' he thought. 'That's an angel singing. I'd better call Molesbury.'

Molesbury, having been the Grimwood family butler for half a century, seemed the ideal man to consult on this occasion. If anybody had heard a singing angel at any time in the last fifty years Molesbury would have been the man to deal with it. He would know exactly what to do.

"Molesbury!" cried Grimwood, so loudly that a layer of dust puffed up from a nearby bound volume of British Birds magazine. "Molesbury! Come quickly!"

He knew this was impossible, of course. Molesbury wasn't a fast mover. Possibly at one time in his butlering youth he had covered a hundred yards in under fifteen minutes, but nowadays he had little chance of achieving such a time. Indeed, when his knee was playing up, it took him two days to travel from one end of the house to the other.

The angel sang again. A simple three-note motif, with a hint of the church bell and an ethereal harmonic or two.

Grimwood looked upwards in wonder, as though expecting to see a host of glowing feathery wings gracefully flitting around the rafters.

Molesbury appeared, having made remarkably good time.

"Molesbury!" said Grimwood. "Did you hear that sound? That strange and beautiful singing!"

"Yes sir," croaked the butler, breathing heavily.

"What do you think it could be? Is it an angel, do you think, calling to us from the golden boughs of heaven?"

"I believe it is the doorbell, sir."

"The doorbell? I didn't know we had a doorbell." Grimwood felt disappointed.

"Nobody has rung the doorbell since the Queen's Jubilee, sir. It was, I recall, a small boy trying to sell us some commemorative cutlery. I sent him on his way, sir, without making a purchase. We had enough cutlery, sir, and I felt no urge to add to our collection."

"I see. Very wise of you. Too much cutlery can be a hardship as well as a blessing. There is the question of storage, for a start, and of course it all needs to be cleaned."

"I appreciate your kind words, sir. It is nice to know my decision was the correct one."

"Indeed. Have the rest of the day off as a reward for your initiative."

"Thank you, sir. The gesture is greatly appreciated."

The doorbell rang again.

"Actually, I suppose you'd better answer that first," said Grimwood.

"Yes, sir. I was on my way to the door when you called me."

"I'll come with you if I may. My mind is boggling, rather."

Grimwood left the library. For a few yards he followed the bent figure of his butler, then having realised it would be quicker to overtake Molesbury and answer the door himself, he put on a burst of speed and reached the door before his loyal servant with seconds to spare.

The bell rang again. Whoever it was, thought Grimwood, was certainly persistent.

He unlatched the huge wooden door and peered outside. A small boy was standing on the step, looking fresh-faced and eager.

"No thank you," said Grimwood hesitantly. "We have enough cutlery. Erm...God Bless the Queen," he added awkwardly, before closing the creaking door. Then he turned to Molesbury, who was now standing at his shoulder. "It's the cutlery boy. He has returned, doubtless hoping we have experienced a change of heart. Nothing more."

"I feel that is unlikely, sir," croaked Molesbury. "I doubt that the young man would have worn his years so lightly."

"Eh?"

"The young man who called on the occasion of the Jubilee would be unlikely still to be a small boy, sir."

"Oh. You mean he'd be a chap by now?"

"Precisely, sir."

"Of course. How silly of me. Well, he must be here for some other reason. What do you think it could be?"

"I could not say, sir. Now I have reached the door I would be happy to engage the visitor in conversation, in order to establish the reason for his visit."

"I'm not sure you could manage the door. It's been a long time since you last opened it. I shall do it. Awfully decent of you to offer, though. Take the rest of the day off."

"Thank you, sir," said Molesbury, not moving.

Grimwood opened the door once more and peered out. The boy was still standing there, sporting a huge grin, the eccentric behaviour of the residents seemingly having done little to dampen his high spirits. He wore a bright red tee-shirt and white shorts that seemed almost luminous. His hair looked as though it had been combed several months ago, but had happily made a full recovery. His permanent smile seemed to fill his whole face, with some left over for passers-by.

"Hello," said Grimwood, attempting to smile back, but feeling his face muscles creak with the effort. "Who are you?"

"I'm your relative," said the boy chirpily.

"I don't have any relatives," said Grimwood.

"I'm your brother's grandson," said the boy. "Jimbo."

"I don't have a brother," said Grimwood. "Certainly not one called 'Jimbo' at any rate."

"No, I'm Jimbo. Your brother was called...well, I just called him Grandad."

"I don't have a brother called Jimbo or Grandad, or anything else," said Grimwood, his smile fading. "Oh…actually, now that you mention it, I do recall someone… small chap, lived in the house with me when I was a child. Grew bigger as the years went by."

"That is the usual pattern of growth, sir," said Molesbury's voice behind him.

"Yes. I did have a brother, didn't I, Molesbury?"

"Yes, sir, His name was actually 'Lupin.' He is two years younger than yourself."

"Lupin! Of course! Lupin, Lupin, Lupin. And what's your name, little boy?"

"Jimbo, sir."

"Jimbo! I've heard that name before somewhere. Now, what are you doing here?"

"I've been sent to spend the summer holidays with you. Grandad's in hospital, mum's in hospital, and there's no-one else to look after me. So it's all come down to you, Grimster! We'll have a great time though won't we? What a super house, and a huge garden. I'm going to have loads of fun here, I can tell."

Grimwood stood and gaped at the small boy, and said nothing. It was all becoming too much for him to take in.

"Who is 'Grimster'?" he asked eventually.

"Well, you are," said Jimbo brightly.

"My name is Grimwood. Is it possible," he said with a hint of hopefulness in his voice, "you have the wrong address?"

"I have a piece of paper. Look."

The small boy took a crumpled piece of paper out of his back pocket and gave it to Grimwood, who handled it gingerly. It didn't look like the kind of thing he enjoyed handling.

The words thereon were clear enough.

'Dear Grimwood, please could you look after James for the summer holidays. There is nowhere else for him to go and we are desperate. It took us ages to find out where you live, but Lupin has told me that you have a big house and a butler so hopefully you have room for him. Thank you, Marion (James's mother).'

Another slight hope took hold of Grimwood.

"Who is James?" he asked, his face brightening slightly. "Not you, I take it?"

"Of course it's me, Grimster!"

"Oh. Jimbo. James. Grimwood. Grimster. I think I'm finally beginning to realise what's going on. You change people's names, doubtless for your own entertainment. Well, I understand the urge. I was a small boy once. I remember the heady excitement that used to overtake me on occasion. Well, you'd better come in. Is that your bag? Splendid." Grimwood felt anything but splendid, but he was a warm-hearted man, and he didn't want to upset the small boy. "Follow me," he added.

Jimbo hopped into the hallway and looked around with wonder.

"Wow," he said after a few seconds. "Look at that dusty old thing."

"That's Molesbury, my butler," said Grimwood. "I'm afraid he doesn't move as quickly as he used to. The dust tends to settle upon his less disturbed surfaces."

"I meant that stag's head," said Jimbo. "Wow! Did you shoot it?"

"What, when it was alive, you mean?"

Jimbo nodded.

"No. Certainly not. It died of natural causes, I think. I don't suppose it was able to eat or drink, what with its head being stuck through a wall. Tell you what er... Jimbo, why don't you go into that room there while I have a quick word with Molesbury? It'll be lunchtime soon."

"Wowsa! Lunchtime. Fantastic."

When Jimbo was out of earshot, Grimwood whispered into his butler's ear.

"Do you think this seems likely? Lupin and all that?"

"No sir, I do not. If you will permit me, I shall walk into the village and make enquiries."

"Can you remember the way? You haven't been for years."

"I'm sure I can, sir. There is a telephone in the candlemaker's shop as I recall."

"Well, go as fast as you can, Molesbury. I only wish I had a car or a bicycle for you."

"The exercise will do me good, sir. It is only half-a-mile to the village. I shall be back in about five hours, sir."

"Knee feeling good, then?"

"Yes, sir. It is in excellent health."

Molesbury, still bent almost double, strode slowly but surely to the large wooden door and closed it laboriously behind him, destroying a shaft of sunlight that had crept into the hallway as he did so.

Chapter 2

There were fourteen chairs at the dining room table, but Grimwood and Jimbo were the only two people present.

"Who else lives here apart from you and Molesbury?" asked Jimbo.

"Nobody, really. Apart from Mrs. Budd, the cook. You'll meet her in a moment," replied Grimwood. "She'll be bringing the mulligatawny soup."

"What's multiganorny soup? I've never had that before."

"It's a kind of soup that tastes of... mulligatawns, I suppose. Yes. Made of mulligatawns. Hence the flavour is very mulligatawny."

"Wow. How do you know it's going to be muliginitawny soup today?"

"It always is. With bread. I don't really like it though."

"Why don't you ask the cook for something different? You could have fish and chips or pizza or jelly or trifle," said Jimbo, licking his lips as he thought of the prospect of all those delicious kinds of food.

"Well, cook doesn't really respond to questioning. She's not very communicative. She has a limited vocabulary," said Grimwood sadly.

"You mean she doesn't say much?"

"Exactly. If she's angry she makes a noise that sounds like 'awwr'. If she's very angry she makes a noise that sounds like 'garww'. If she's furious, a 'wrgghhhhhhhh' escapes her lips. That's all, really."

"What if she's not angry?"

"I've never known of such a thing," said Grimwood. "She is angry. It is her natural state." He shuffled nervously. "I suspect she was born angry. Oh, er… here she comes now," he said, lowering his head fearfully.

A very large and very square woman dressed in a filthy apron entered the room and looked at Jimbo with a mixture of bemusement and horror.

"Garww," she said.

"Hello, Mrs. Budd. This is Jimbo. He's staying with us for the holidays."

"Garww," she said again.

"I'm not sure I want mulletgorblimey soup," said Jimbo. "Could I have steak and kidney pie instead, please?"

"Awwr," said Mrs Budd and stormed out of the room. She returned a few moments later pushing an old rusty trolley, which held two bowls of soup and a crust of bread. She tore the latter viciously into two pieces with her claw-like hands.

"Thank you," said Jimbo, not forgetting his manners despite his disappointment.

Mrs. Budd bustled off, her every movement exuding barely-controlled fury. Jimbo tasted the soup.

"It's very watery," he said, wrinkling his nose.

"Yes it is. I doubt there are very many mulligatawns in it," admitted Grimwood.

"The bread's stale as well."

"Yes. It always is. It's really more of a building material than a foodstuff."

"Do you pay the cook? Are you her boss?"

"Yes, I do. Sorry, I mean yes, I am."

"Shouldn't she do nicer food then, if you ask for it?"

"Yes. To be honest though, Jimbo, myself and Molesbury are absolutely terrified of her. She's very large. You saw what she did to the stale bread. You could imagine what she could do with Molesbury, who is less resistant to force."

Jimbo gave Grimwood a cheeky smile.

"Mrs. Budd!" he cried, much to Grimwood's horror. "Come here please!"

Grimwood gestured at him to be silent, and slunk down in his chair as Mrs. Budd returned, her many-chinned face set in a violent sneer.

"Hello again, Mrs. Budd," said Jimbo. "This soup is okay today, but tomorrow me and Grimwood would like steak and kidney pie followed by jelly and ice cream please. Or even vanilla custard! Wouldn't we, Grimwood?"

Grimwood had left his chair and was hiding under the table. All Jimbo could see of him was a tuft of greying hair, which appeared to be quivering with fright.

"Wrgghhhhhhhh!" said Mrs. Budd, moving towards Jimbo with a terrifying gleam in her eye, flexing her muscles as though about to show some stale bread who was the boss.

It was a shame that at this stage Grimwood decided to move even further under the table, as he missed a quite remarkable display of agility from his young house-guest. Firstly Jimbo leapt onto the surface of the table, causing his mulligatawny soup to jump temporarily from its bowl. When this still wasn't enough to shake off the advance of the cook, he leapt even higher and grabbed a chandelier, which started rocking violently from side to side. His feet now waving about indiscriminately, Jimbo became a danger to all personnel, and the cook found her attempts to grab his legs thwarted by flying steel-capped boots. Abandoning this technique, she started throwing chunks of stale bread at Jimbo's head in an attempt to make him loosen his grip and return to the more conventionally occupied areas of the dining room. Luckily her aim was poor. Her positioning was also poor, as Jimbo's swinging legs accidentally caught her in the small of the back as she bent to grab more ammunition from the plate of bread on the trolley. This caused her to fall chest first onto the trolley, which, finding itself carrying an unexpected weight travelling with momentum, rolled back through the door into the corridor, carrying the cook's body with it, her little legs dangling in mid-air. At this stage the ceiling finally gave way, depositing Jimbo and the chandelier on the table together with several pounds of plaster and a cloud of dust that covered everything within sight.

At this stage Grimwood left his safe haven and peered into the room to survey the damage.

"Are you in good health, Jimbo?" he asked.

"Oh yes. Bruised my knee a bit. Sorry about the ceiling. We've got a bit of dust in the soup as well. Did you see Mrs. Budd zoom out of the room on that trolley? It was ever so funny."

"I'm afraid I was not lucky enough to witness the spectacle." Grimwood paused for a moment. "Was the trolley travelling at speed?"

"Oh yes," chortled Jimbo.

"Really? Well I say, what? Such a shame I dropped my spoon under the table. I would have liked to have assisted you in your battle against the forces of darkness, but it wasn't to be. There is a lot of dust, isn't there? It reminds me of the time Molesbury sneezed."

"Yes. We can clear it up later. We'll have to go out for some grub though, now," said Jimbo. "There's a cafe in the village that sells ice cream and fizzy cans."

Grimwood looked uneasy at the prospect. "I haven't eaten outside of Dunnydark Hall for well over a quarter of a century," he said. "I have no intention of doing so."

"Okay," said Jimbo, disappointed. "I suppose we could try and get the dust out of the soup. Or maybe we should leave it in. It will improve the flavour." He picked up a spoon and stirred the dusty soup thoughtfully. "Why do you never leave the Hall?"

Grimwood contemplated the question, lowering his brow as he did so. "It seems such a waste of effort to go out," he said eventually. "I'd only end up coming back in again."

"If you were full of ice cream and fizzy drinks, you'd have bags of energy."

"You consider these foods to have a remedial effect upon the body's vital organs?"

"They'll give you plenty of kazoom."

"Then I shall try them," said Grimwood bravely, feeling a little like a man about to jump out of a plane with a second-hand parachute. "Take me to this cafe of which you speak. I have never had kazoom before, but I like to think I am open to new experiences, as long as they only come along every fifty years or so. We must move quickly though, before Mrs. Budd returns to wreak havoc upon us."

Chapter 3

Grimwood looked about him and narrowed his eyes. The world outside Dunnydark Hall seemed awfully bright - much brighter and more colourful than he remembered it. It was a long time since he'd been outside, and he became conscious that he was overdressed for the warm weather. He watched Jimbo running ahead of him and wondered why the child didn't catch fire, so quickly did he seem to move under the glare of the sun. His thoughts were interrupted by a cry from the youngster, who had passed the gates that marked the end of the drive and the beginning of the public road.

"Hey, Grimster! Your butler's here. Whassisname. Molesbury."

Grimwood shuffled closer and saw that Molesbury was indeed lying by the side of the road, bent into an almost perfect arch. Tremendously worried, Grimwood rushed forward to speak to his man, despite feeling sweaty and uncomfortable after the unaccustomed exercise.

"Molesbury! Are you alright?"

"Yes sir. Thank you for asking, sir."

"What are you doing on the ground?"

"I'm afraid I am not used to the force of the wind outside the hall, sir. I have been blown over. However, I doubt I have incurred serious injury, and I am able to resume my usual duties, sir."

"As soon as you can stand up, you mean?"

"Yes, sir. I regret to say that I may need some assistance doing so. I have been awaiting a passing member of the peasantry, sir."

"Myself and Jimbo can assist."

"I would be very grateful, sir. I'm sure you understand that it is not in my nature to seek such assistance from my employer, but circumstances are exceptional."

"Of course. Don't concern yourself about such things, Molesbury. I promise I do not think any less of you."

Grimwood and Jimbo rolled the prostrate butler onto his back, and then, each of them taking an arm, hauled the old man back into his usual position.

"Thank you, sirs. I am most grateful. I fear that, having missed my mulligatawny soup this lunchtime, my constitution was unable to cope with the wind, which, as you have no doubt noticed, is a stiff south-westerly. I shall rest on that bench for a moment, sir. May I ask why you are in the vicinity? It is most unlike yourself to leave the Hall, sir."

"Well, Jimbo upset cook, and she ended up on the trolley heading, like the wind, in a south-westerly direction, that is away from the dining-room and into the corridor. Doubtless she found that the corridor did not have any soup making facilities therein, and as a consequence we have found ourselves forced to forage for food. The young man has recommended an eating establishment in the village where I believe we will be able to refuel."

"Ice-cream, cakes, everything," said Jimbo. "Are you coming with us?"

"I fear my strength insufficient, sir," replied Molesbury sadly.

"We'll bring you some back, Moley," said Jimbo.

"Yes. I suppose we could," said Grimwood. "Wait there. We'll feed you something heavy to act as ballast," he added, kindly.

Molesbury nodded in a dignified way as his companions went on with their journey.

Grimwood stood at the threshold of 'Ye Olde Nooke Teashop' and swallowed hard. In order to reach the hallowed establishment he had already been forced to cross two roads, one of which had a car on it.

"Wasn't it funny when that car beeped his horn at you, Grimmy!" said Jimbo with a light laugh. "I think he wanted you to cross the road a bit quicker."

"I am unaccustomed to the pace of life in the metropolis, Jimbo," said Grimwood. "It is a long time since I ventured into the centre of Little Ducking. The village has doubled in size since I was younger, and the traffic has intensified. There are several more ducks on the pond as well. I had heard that the pace of modern life was pretty frantic, but it is still a shock when you experience it in the flesh. Should we wait here to be seated?"

"No, just grab a chair. I want to sit here by the window."

"I bow to your expertise in such matters. You are clearly a bon viveur, and a regular in such establishments."

Jimbo sat down and immediately caught the eye of a waitress.

"Cooee!" called Jimbo, shrilly. "Can I have a big bowl of ice-cream, please? Don't spare the wafers. What are you having, Grimmychops?"

There was a pause. The waitress bore little physical resemblance to Mrs. Budd and was very different in demeanour, having a big friendly smile that warmed the whole room. She stared at Grimwood expectantly.

"Would you like a cold drink, sir? It's warm outside and you're a bit overdressed in all those tweeds. You're looking a bit red in the face. Why don't I fetch you a nice glass of sparkling water?"

"Sparkling?" said Grimwood, bemused.

"Yes. You know, fizzy," said the waitress.

"Fizzy water?" asked Grimwood. "I'm afraid I may not be ready for such a thing. I shall have water from the tap please. Do you sell mulligatawny soup? No? Oh."

"Have a nice plate of pie and chips, Grimmy," suggested Jimbo.

"We do a lovely shepherd's pie," said the waitress with a grin.

"I could have that, I suppose. Would the shepherd mind, do you think?"

"I don't think he'll mind at all," said the waitress winking at Jimbo. "We'll keep another one in the kitchen for him."

"Splendid. In that case, I shall allow my adventurous instincts to take over. Bring on the pie. Wheel it in. It shall be consumed."

"Fizzy cola for me please as well!" said Jimbo, as the waitress turned to leave. "Cor, Grimmy, this is going to be fantastic."

The waitress returned and placed a huge bowl of ice cream in front of Jimbo.

"Shouldn't a growing lad like yourself be eating vegetables, or some such thing?" asked Grimwood, eyeing his companion's lunch with mistrust.

"You know that game called 'Animal, Vegetable or Mineral?' asked Jimbo between mouthfuls of pink ice-cream.

"Yes," said Grimwood, wondering why the child had changed the topic so abruptly. "I played it as a youngster."

"Well, it works because everything in the world is animal, vegetable or mineral."

"Yes. Your words are true."

"Well, is ice-cream an animal?"

"No."

"Is it a mineral?"

"I'd say not."

"Well, it must be a vegetable then."

"My word, I think you are right. Your logic is unassailable. Tuck in. Make sure you eat up the whole bowl, mind, if you want to grow up big and strong.

Perhaps we should take some back for Molesbury as well. He could do with an injection of good healthy vegetables."

"It'll melt."

"Will it? Shame. Oh, here's my pie. Is it mine? Yes!"

Grimwood prepared himself psychologically by having a sip of the tap water - which, he thought, tasted rather like Mrs Budd's mulligatawny soup - before sticking his fork into his meal and tasting.

For a few moments he was unable to think or speak. He felt as if he had dived into an ocean of scented flowers. Eventually a whimper of purest pleasure escaped him.

"Is it good, then?" asked Jimbo, slurping ice cream.

"My goodness. Goodness me. Yes. Marvellous."

"Excuse me," said Jimbo shrilly to the waitress when she reappeared from the kitchen. "Who cooked the pie?"

"I did," she said with a sudden look of concern. "I do everything here. Anything wrong?"

"Would you like to come and work at Dunnydark Hall? Grimster will pay you double what you make now, won't you Grimster?"

"What? What? Will I?"

"Of course you will," said Jimbo.

"Well, you've asked at just the right moment," said the waitress, beaming. "I've been running this teashop on my own for five years and I'm just about to pack the whole thing up. Thank you so much for your kind offer. I accept!"

"Just think, Grimmy!" shouted Jimbo. "Shepherd's pie, shepherd's pie, shepherd's pie, every day more shepherd's pie! Better buy some bigger trousers!"

"Excusing me, please," said a pleasant looking woman dressed in a bright orange tee-shirt at the next table. "Did I hear you were saying that you were living at the Dunnydark Hall? The greatest big house in the area of the county, yes?"

"What? Where? Who? Wherefore?" said Grimwood, turning his head this way and that, trying to keep track of events.

"We, the thing is me and my girlfriends, we are in the England glancing around by the country houses. We were seeing your house with all the signs saying 'private' and 'please be keeping away.' Could we arrive and be admiring of your house we are thinking it may be good?"

"What? Why? Whereby?" said Grimwood.

"Course you can!" said Jimbo. "Grimmy would love having some ladies in the house wouldn't you, Grimmychops?"

"W... w... w... Would I?"

"Is great! Thanking you so much. These are being my girlfriends, Halana and Halana." She indicated two more smiling women of a similar age, also in orange tee-shirts, who had appeared from the corridor leading to the toilets. "My name is Halana too. We are all being named Halana. It is a little bit crazy, for sure, yes? We are Halana and there is the three of us. We are arriving from the Netherlands, for sure. You are a sweet little boy. What are they naming you?"

"People call me all sorts of names. My real name is Jimbo. You can stay if you like. Grimmychops has plenty of spare rooms."

Halana's eyes widened and she looked at Grimwood as if he were a knight in shining armour and she a damsel who had just been rescued from a particularly bad-mannered dragon. "You'd do that, Grimmychops? Is so sweet. I'm going to kiss you I think, for sure now." She leant over and kissed Grimwood on the cheek, just above the whisker line. Grimwood reddened and made some incoherent noises. "We'll be dropping on laters. Let's be coming on, Halana and Halana, is now time to be going!" The three Dutch women grabbed their rucksacks and filed out of the cafe, each Halana pausing to kiss Grimwood on the top of his head on the way out.

"Wow," said Jimbo. "I bet they'll be good fun. Eat your pie up, Grimmy, it'll go cold."

Chapter 4

After Jimbo had cheerfully and unexpectedly paid the bill - Grimwood finding that the pound note he had upon his person was no longer considered legal tender - they returned to find Molesbury exactly where they had left him, a serene smile upon the butler's face.

"I am pleased you have returned, sir. The day is a pleasant one, stiff breeze notwithstanding, but nonetheless I was beginning to lack intellectual stimulation. There has been a beetle running hither and thither in my vicinity, but apart from that I have been quite alone."

"As bored as a very bored badger in other words," said Jimbo. "Don't blame you, Moley. We've brought you some lemon cake." He held out a slice, wrapped in sticky paper, which Molesbury accepted with dignity.

"It's rather marvellous, Molesbury," said Grimwood. "Made of pure vegetables. It will put some power into your old bones."

Molesbury tasted the cake, and his face lit up with the kind of joy that few elderly butlers are lucky enough to have experienced.

"It certainly does seem to have the effect of refreshing the internal organs, sir. Both texture and taste give undiluted pleasure. Oh, by the way, sir, I was passed half-an-hour ago by Mrs. Budd. She gave me this letter which I believe I am expected to pass on to you, sir."

"What does it say?"

"I shall read it aloud, sir, once this last remaining piece of cake has been successfully placed into the care of my digestive system."

"No rush, Molesbury."

"I believe I am ready now, sir. I am invigorated. I shall need to wipe my fingers, sir." He did so. "I am now ready to read, sir."

"Splendid. Read it with as much verve and feeling as you can muster."

"The note reads thusly, sir. 'Wrgghhhhhhh! I'm off!'"

"I see. She has obviously experienced strong emotions. I never knew she had such a broad vocabulary. May I read the note? I've always wondered how to spell 'wrgghhhhhhh'. It is a word I have heard her use on a couple of occasions."

"Of course, sir. I believe it was intended for your eyes anyway. You will note there are seven specimens of the letter 'h', sir."

Jimbo, who had grown rather bored during this long exchange and had been trying to train the beetle to sit up and beg for cake crumbs, suddenly burst into the conversation.

"It doesn't matter if she's gone. Grimwood offered the woman at the cafe a job, and she's accepted."

"Is that true, sir?" asked Molesbury gravely.

"Er… yes. Yes, it is true. I decided that action needed to be taken, vis-a-vis the staff. Time to sweep out the old broom with a new... erm... broom. Fresh legs. "

"An excellent decision, I'm sure, sir"

"And there are three Dutchy ladies coming as well, all called Halana, and all pretty," added Jimbo happily.

"Is that true, sir?" asked Molesbury, even more gravely.

"Jimbo," said Grimwood after contemplating the question for a few moments. "You'd better run off back to Dunnydark. Myself and Molesbury will hold you up. You're full of the joys of spring and summer and whatnot, and your legs refuse to be stilled. Here's the key. We shall follow on behind. Keep away from that tree! The one with the fence round it. Out of bounds. Forbidden."

"Wow! What a big key. It looks like a cricket bat! Wheeeee!" said Jimbo, ignoring the instructions regarding the tree completely. "Hurrah! Summertime!" he added, and with these words of wisdom he was away, racing for the door, waving the key aloft as if it were a small sword.

"I take it you sent the young gentleman ahead in order to gain my ear, sir," said Molesbury.

"I certainly did," replied Molesbury. "As you know, Molesbury, I'm normally the most sensible of men. However, the presence of Jimbo is greatly reducing my ability to reason. He moves and speaks so quickly that I find myself struggling to get a grip on the prevailing circumstances. He has invited a waitress in the cafe to replace Mrs. Budd, and he has told the three Halanas that

31

they can stay under my roof. We haven't had guests since the... er... Bad Thing happened, have we Molesbury? I'm not sure I can face them. My nervous system has been through the mangle today. The last few hours have been a melange of new experiences and excitement."

"A melange, sir?"

"Yes. A melange. Rather a lovely word, isn't it, Molesbury?"

"It gives me a certain pleasure to hear it used, sir. I can not deny it."

"Excellent. I may use it again at some time in the future, if the fancy takes me. Now, where was I?"

"Facing a melange of new experiences and excitements, sir."

"Oh yes. Thank you, Molesbury. Anyway, I was about to say that I had decided some time ago that myself and the world wouldn't get on, yet I have been forced to re-acquaint myself with the bally thing."

"I take it you ate at the cafe, sir?" said Molesbury, who had started to blow over in the wind again. Thankfully Grimwood was on hand to manoeuvre him back into an upright position before he reached the ground.

"Steady, Molesbury! Yes, we did. Shepherd's pie, Molesbury. The food of the Gods! Even the tap water tasted like nectar."

"So the replacement of Mrs. Budd with the new lady is something to be applauded, sir?"

"I suppose it is. I still think we need to find out if the young ragamuffin is who he says he is, though. Doubts remain within me. Shame you couldn't make the phone. I shall sneak off to the village later myself. Do you know phone boxes aren't red any more, Molesbury?"

"You shock me, sir."

"Indeed. Still, that's progress I suppose. Things that were once red are red no longer. Anyway, we'd better sort the spare rooms out. The whole place will be crawling with Halanas before you know it. Doubtless they'll be eating snails or morris dancing or kissing the Blarneystone or some such horror. I shall have to remind them that this is... erm..."

"England, sir."

"England. Precisely. And when they are in Rome, they must do as the Romans do."

"You express yourself very well and clearly, sir."

They walked the short distance back to the front door, Grimwood holding onto Molesbury's arm as they did so to prevent further tumbles.

"In you go, old man," said Grimwood, guiding the butler inside. "Where's Jimbo? He's not in the hallway. Where has the little fellow escaped to?"

Jimbo suddenly appeared, his bright clothes and endless smile in stark contrast to the colourless hallway.

"I've been in your library. Wow! It's full of books about birdies. What birdies do you get here? We had a Greatly Spotted Woodenpecker in our garden once. Grandad told me what it was. I'll bet you get loads of birds here, don't you? All big, noisy and colourful ones. Do you have any bonicliers?

"You mean binoculars, perchance?"

"Yes. Binocliers."

"No. I'm afraid if I have a pair about the house they will be somewhat antique, and rather dirty. I still read about birdies... I mean birds, but I'm afraid I've rather lost the will to go outside and look at them. It seems such an effort."

"We can set up a bird table. I've still got some cake from the tea shop. Look, over here!" Jimbo dragged Grimwood over to a small patch of lawn near the front door, surrounded by rhododendron bushes. "See, it's nice and sheltered here. Look! There's a blackbird, and some little brown things. Oops, they've flown away. Do you have a bird table?"

"No."

"Anything a few feet tall with a flat bit you could put the cake on?"

"Nothing springs immediately to mind. Having said that, nothing really springs into my mind at all these days. Things tend to crawl slowly into my mind, like slugs. Not a very nice image, I know, but an accurate one. Particularly since once a thing has entered my mind, it tends to crawl about in there for some time, making a nuisance of itself."

"I believe I can be of assistance, sir," said Molesbury, who had creaked into the picture. "As sir may well have noticed, I have rather a hunched profile. If the young gentleman were to put the cake crumbs on my back, I'm sure I would prove an attractive proposition to the local avifauna, sir."

"Aviwhatty?" said Jimbo.

34

"Avifauna, young sir. Birdlife."

"Wow! Wouldn't you blow over again?"

"The possibility is always with us, young sir. However, as you have observed, the area is a sheltered one."

"Wouldn't you scare the birds away?"

"I am capable of a great and profound stillness that permeates both body and soul, young sir. I once practised the art of yoga. Please remember that I am also fortified with cake."

"Wow! Go on then. Stand there. I'll sprinkle the crumbs on."

"What? Wherefore? You can't do this! Can you?" spluttered Grimwood.

"I live only to serve, sir," said Molesbury.

"What? I..."

"Best go in before nightfall, Moley!" cooed Jimbo. "You could get rats."

"Get rats?" said Grimwood, who was beginning to feel that, once again, the situation was beginning to slip from his grasp. "Get rats? Molesbury's never had rats in his life, have you, Molesbury?"

"No, sir. I am fortunate not to have experienced that particular infestation. May I suggest that the young sir fetches a few more breadcrumbs from the kitchen? They will no doubt be stale, yet I am sure they will be satisfactory for the needs of the avifauna."

"Wow. What a fab butler you are, Moley. Byeee!" Jimbo ran off in the direction of the house, beaming with happiness.

"I think, sir, that this would be a good time to return to the village and make th one call. Whilst the young gentleman is occupied, you understand, sir."

"What? Whither? Yes! Of course! How clever of you, Moley. I mean Molesbury. Yes, I see. I'll go straight away. Not a moment to lose, eh? Seize the moment, that's the ticket. Strike while the ironing's hot. Carp thingy."

" I would advise haste, sir."

"Yes. Right. No time like the present. Speed of thought and foot is of the essence. Back to the village. Off I go."

With those decisive words, Grimwood left his ever-faithful butler and headed away down the drive.

Chapter 5

Grimwood had nearly reached the main gates when he was greeted by the sight of the three Halanas and a young man approaching.

"Grimmychops!" shouted the first Halana, and rushed up to hug him. "Thanking you so much for the letting of us into your house, certainly for sure. Your name is strange, yes?"

"What?" said Grimwood, feeling himself blushing.

"We are bringing Ulf. He and Halana are courting, and they have been kissing many times. I am thinking they will be married soon."

"Oh Halana, you are being extremely crazy," said Halana, laughing.

Ulf said nothing. He was very tall, but he seemed a shy young man, reluctant to make eye contact. There was a pair of binoculars around his neck.

"Ulf is Norwegian. He is here spying on the deers and the wildlife, and he is seeing Halana and thinking she is so very nice."

"Oh Halana, stop with the crazy silly talk!" urged Halana.

They all laughed. Ulf looked embarrassed. "I have not seen any deer or wildlife. I did not expect to, because in general I am a very unlucky person," he said glumly.

"Well, I have to go to the village," said Grimwood, in a moment of decisiveness. "I will be back soon."

"Oh no, Grimmychops!" said Halana. "You must show us our rooms first. Come on Halanas!" The other two Halanas grabbed an arm apiece and gently steered Grimwood back towards the house. "We are not being so long. We are all loving you so much, Grimmychops, for the letting of your house and the bedding and the breakfasting."

Ulf, however, remained a few yards behind, looking at something through his binoculars.

"Grimmychops," he said eventually, in a strong Norwegian accent. "There appears to be a very old man standing in your garden with a piece of cake on his back. I can also see a small boy watching him from the bushes. It is rather a strange and depressing sight."

"What? Why? Oh yes. Take no notice. Where did you say you were from? Norway? Not the kind of thing you see much of over there, I would think. Fjords - they are called fjords, aren't they? Yes? Fjords are very spectacular, of course, and attract a lot of tourists, but butler-bird tables more or less unknown in all probability. Just ignore it. If you ignore it, it will ignore you. Erm... for sure."

"But there is now a bird on the butler's back, pecking at the cake!"

"Well, why shouldn't it? You can't leave cake lying around in a garden and expect birds not to eat it. I'm sure the vegetables therein will do it a power of good. Give it a bit of lift."

"It is a strange bird. One I have not seen before."

"Well, you're in a different country. Sure to be some birds over here you haven't met before."

"Be leaving him to his birds," said a Halana. "If you are now to be showing us of the rooms that would be very fantastic."

"What? Yes. Of course. This way." Grimwood had a smile on his face. A small smile, but a smile nonetheless.

Ulf had an idea. He took out his mobile phone and called up a man he had met earlier in the week.

"Jeremy?" he said. "You asked me to tell you if I saw anything interesting. Well, I have done, although knowing my luck it will be flying a long way away very soon."

Grimwood showed the three Halanas the guest rooms, all of which were tidy but dusty, as though they hadn't been used for well over a decade.

"I'm afraid these rooms haven't been used for a very long time," he admitted. "Nothing wrong with them though. Just brush the dust off. I was going to tidy them earlier, but the time became filled with other things."

"Are there being the spiders?" asked the only Halana who had not yet spoken until this point. "I am hating the spiders with their such long legs and sticking webs. I am thinking that if the spider is to be walking on me, I am screaming and waving my hands about as a crazy person, for sure."

"Well, there is the odd spider, but they tend to keep themselves to themselves. We don't poke our noses into their affairs and, generally speaking, they don't poke their noses into ours. Do spiders have noses?" pondered Grimwood.

"I am hoping not to get so close to one of them that I am looking up its nose."

"For the best, I would imagine. I suspect there are things up spiders noses that would make strong men tremble at the knees. Anyway, make yourselves at home."

Grimwood retired into his own room and shut the door.

"Hang the village and the phone. They'll have to wait," he murmured to himself before collapsing onto his bed. It had been the busiest day of the second half of his life, and he had felt the life-force draining away from him as the afternoon wore on, reducing his ability to think his way out of the problem. The presence of a large shepherd's pie in his belly also added to the general feeling of weariness that now overwhelmed him, and in a few moments he had entered the gentle world of sleep.

When he awoke, half way through an evening that had become cool and still, he immediately became aware of a strange noise outside. It consisted of a curious mixture of clicks, whirrs and gentle whispering; a bizarre aural concoction that Grimwood could make nothing of whatsoever. Stretching, he rose and looked out of the window, and saw to his horror a crowd of about three hundred people, all apparently strangers to him, standing on his front lawn. They were mainly men, and all had either a camera or a telescope. Every optical device was pointed in the same direction, this being the place in which the splendid Molesbury had placed himself for the benefit of the local birdlife.

Grimwood rushed downstairs. His first response was to shout at everyone to clear off, but a sort of shyness prevailed and he decided to join the ranks of strangers and ascertain for himself what was going on. He eventually found a man who seemed to have a friendlier and more relaxed face than many of his fellows, and engaged him in conversation.

"Excuse me. Could you tell me why you are all here?"

"Rare bird. Slate-Coloured Junco. It's from America."

"America? Why would it come here?"

"Blown off course, I suppose. It's on that bird table. The one shaped like a hunched old man. You'd think it was a hunched old man, if it wasn't for the dust. Here, have a look through my telescope."

"Why, thank you. Don't mind if I do."

Grimwood looked. Sure enough, a strange bird was feeding on the cake crumbs. It was mainly blueish-grey with a startling white belly. It certainly didn't resemble anything Grimwood had seen in his bird books, which he spent a lot of time reading. He was really quite excited. He had always loved birds, and if it hadn't been for the sad circumstances in which he had found himself, he was sure he would have spent a lot of time in the great outdoors chasing Juncos of every hue. Nonetheless, he felt obliged to ask a rather important question.

"Do you have permission to be here, by the way?"

"Well, there's a little boy, says he lives here. He told us all we could come in and have a look. So who knows? He could be right or he could be wrong. I'll just stay here until someone throws us off. Oh, look, here he comes now."

Jimbo, clearly not feeling any need to whisper, came bounding up to Grimwood, with a red bucket in one hand and the other flailing in wild excitement, causing a couple of the twitchers to turn around and tut-tut at him disapprovingly.

"Grimbo!" he shouted. "There's a Slightly Coloured Junkie on Moley and all these birdtwitchers have turned up. Me and Ulf took a collection for the house and look how much money we've raised!"

Grimwood peered into the bucket. It was filled with notes and coinage of every description.

"Well! What!"

"It's for the upkeep of Dunnyduck. You can do the place up a bit. Mend the hole in the kitchen ceiling."

"There isn't a hole in the kitchen... oh yes, so there is. Silly me."

Grimwood looked around. New cars were arriving all the time, each discharging more birdwatchers, some of whom ran to the crowd almost breathless with excitement. He took the bucket off Jimbo and placed it carefully by his feet.

He heard cries of "Is it showing?" and "Is it still there?" but they didn't really register with him.

"Yes, the hole in the ceiling," he said absent-mindedly. "Yes, I'm the owner, I suppose. Do the place up. Of course. Rather a lot of money in the bucket, if I ever need it. It is possible I may, if my pound notes are no longer legal currency."

"Excuse me," said a bony-faced twitcher a few yards away. "I'm afraid I couldn't help but overhear. Did I hear you say you were the owner of Dunnydark?"

"What? Who? Me?"

"Yes!" said Jimbo. "This is Grimblechops. He owns the whole ruddy place and all the garden and the trees and the butler and everything. He's as rich as a rich tea biscuit."

"Well, erm... Grimblechops... you could really help us out. I'm the president of the local dramatic society. We were supposed to be doing 'A Midsummer Night's Dream' in Royal Park next week but there's been an outbreak of badgers and we've had to cancel the performance. I don't suppose we could use your lovely house and grounds, could we? Just for one night. We won't be any trouble. We will of course make a donation to help you do the old place up a bit. I understand there's a lake at the back. That would make a lovely backdrop."

"An outbreak of badgers?" said Grimwood in utter confusion.

"Yes. They've dug up the outdoor theatre area looking for worms or bulbs or something."

"Buried badger treasure for pirate badgers," suggested Jimbo, but no-one took any notice of him.

"You want to do it here?" said Grimwood.

Grimwood's old heart softened. During his long self-imposed imprisonment he had lost the knack of confrontation and argument. It seemed so much easier just to agree, and let this pleasant bony-faced man return to eyeing up the rare bird, which he had previously been doing with obvious enjoyment. He quite fancied another look through his telescope as well, and hoped that if relationships remained cordial he would be permitted to have one.

"Yes," he grunted. "Yes, I suppose so."

"Oo! Oo!" said Jimbo, jumping up and down with both hands in the air. "Can I play Macbeth?"

Chapter 6

When Grimwood awoke the next morning, things were, as always, reassuringly quiet. There was the odd tootle from a bird about its business in the grounds, but apart from that, nothing. As was the wont of any bird-lover, he found himself idly wondering what the identity of the tootler could be, and as he did so a series of nightmarish visions and remembrances flooded into his brain, making him shudder and causing his skin to prickle.

At that moment the door creaked open and the hunched figure of Molesbury slouched into the room carrying a cup of tea on a silver tray. Because of his horizontal posture the tray could not have been more than two feet off the ground.

"Ah! Molesbury!"

"Good morning, sir."

"Molesbury, I must tell you, I had the most remarkable dream. It involved a boy called Jumbo. Lovely tea, by the way," he said, taking a sip. "Just the way I like it. Hot enough but just about cold enough."

"Thank you, sir. Did you say Jumbo, sir?"

"Yes. Jumbo. He came around claiming to be my brother, and before you know it there was a rare bird on your back and three Dutch girls called Halana eating cake. It's all a bit confused now, but that was the gist of it. Must have been an overdose of mulligatawny soup I suppose. Did we have an extra large bowl of it for supper? I can't remember. Anyway, no harm done, t'was but a dream. On with life in all its glorious quietness and predictability."

Suddenly, the peace was broken by Jimbo running into the room, his arms outstretched as though he was pretending to be an aeroplane. The effect was enhanced by a series of bizarre noises that, Grimwood thought, seemed to be coming from the general area of his lips.

"Brrrrrrrrrrrrrrrrzzzzzz Cheu cheu deyyyyyaaaaaaa-aaaaaaaaa kapoom kapoom!" said Jimbo.

"Sweet Lord in heaven!" exclaimed Grimwood, dropping the thankfully now empty teacup from his hands. It balanced precariously for a moment on his bedspread, then gave up its small battle for balance and tinkled onto the floor, losing its handle in the process.

"Molesbury," said Grimwood in a croaking tone, as Jimbo continued his aircraft impression. "Am I awake?"

"I believe so, sir."

"How can you be so sure?"

"You will notice that you have consumed a cup of tea, sir. This is an example of behaviour which is not usually performed by those who are asleep."

"Could I have dreamt it? Could I be dreaming this boy? The one currently flying around my room, creating a variety of sounds? Were the events I recall rooted in the soil of reality?"

"A pleasant turn of phrase, if I may say so, sir."

"Thank you." There was a moment's silence, or there would have been, had Jimbo not been dive-bombing an aspidistra in a pot near the windowsill.

"I'm sure I just asked you a question, Molesbury, but I can't remember what it was. Are there thousands of people with binoculars outside?"

"No, sir. Regrettably, the bird was taken by a cat towards dusk last night, sir. Word has spread rapidly amongst the birdwatching fraternity and the grounds are once more twitcher-free, sir."

"I see. Halanas?"

"Yet to arise, sir."

"Elf?"

"Ulf is yet to arise, sir."

"Titania?"

"There is no-one by that name on the premises as far as I am aware, sir. The only Titania I know is a character in a Midsummer Night's Dream, sir, which as you are aware is a play by Shakespeare."

"Of course. They're performing it by the lake next week. I was getting confused. I do, occasionally."

"You are unfair to yourself, sir. Your mind is still as sharp as a shoe."

"Thank you, Molesbury."

"Not at all, sir."

"Take the rest of the day off."

"Aaaaaaaaaaaaaaaaaaaaaaaaaaaaaaaaaaaargh!"

"I'm sorry Molesbury? What was that?"

"I did not speak, sir. I merely bowed gently in a deferential manner."

"I could have sworn you said 'aaaaaaaaaaa-aaaaaaaaaaaargh'.

"No, sir. That was Jimbo. You will no doubt be able to observe that, in the midst of his aeroplane impersonation, he failed to notice the open window. He has fallen out of it."

"So he has! My word! Will he be injured, do you think?"

"I think it unlikely, sir. There is a large pile of grass cuttings and other garden waste beneath the window. You remember the gardening men came last week. Jimbo will have had a soft landing."

"Nonetheless, perhaps we ought to go and have a look."

"It may be prudent, sir."

Grimwood left the sanctuary of his bed and reached the window before his butler. He looked downwards and saw a pile of grass cuttings imprinted with the prostrate figure of Jimbo, arms still outstretched, face upwards, giggling helplessly.

"Jimbo! Are you in good health?" demanded Grimwood.

"Oo, yes, thanks Grimbo! Though I think there's a thistle stuck in my bottom."

"Need we call an ambulance?"

"You can if you like. I like the sirens. Eee-uuuu eee-uuuuu. Who for?"

"Why, for you of course!"

Jimbo giggled again, then leapt up and clambered down onto the path. He jumped up and down a couple of times, then span round a couple of times and fell over.

"Not for me. I'm fine. Wowsa. Lumme jumpers!" He resumed his aeroplane act, this time with rather more space to express himself. In a few moments he had reached a large horse chestnut tree and was attacking it with his propellers.

"I believe he will make a full recovery, sir," said Molesbury.

"Molesbury?"

"Yes, sir?"

"You will make an effort to reach the village again today, will you? To make the phone call?"

"As a matter of some urgency, sir. The day is very calm. I foresee no obstacle."

As Grimwood descended the stairs he was surprised to hear the doorbell ring yet again. He shook off the idea that it was another boy come to sell him commemorative cutlery, and, Molesbury being still busy upstairs, decided to answer it himself.

There was a stranger at the door. He wore a dark suit and an even darker coat, and had a smile that was more frightening than most people's snarls.

"Good morning," said the stranger. "Though I would like to stress that by 'Good Morning' I make no inference or guarantee that the morning is good. It is merely a commonly used form of greeting, frequently encountered in polite society. My name is Marmaduke Gibbon."

"I'm very sorry to hear that," said Grimwood, who was by no means immune to the suffering of others. "Why are you here?"

"I am here in my capacity as a representative of the firm of Gibbon, Gibbon, Gibbon and Gibbon. My client, on whose business I am here today, is Mrs. Belinda Budd." The stranger carried a large briefcase, which was obviously heavy and gave him a lopsided appearance. His other hand fidgeted in a rather unpleasant way, the bony fingers twining around each other like skinny pink worms.

"That's awfully nice of you. Who is she?" said Grimwood, trying not to be distracted by the constant motion of the hand.

"I am given to understand that Mrs. Budd had, until yesterday, the... er... twentieth of July, been in your service as a cook and general housekeeper."

"Oh. Yes, I suppose so," said Grimwood, who, after a good night's sleep, was feeling very acute mentally. "Although the word 'cook' is putting a bit strongly. She sort of bimbled about in the kitchen like a lost ox, producing mulligatawny soup at regular intervals. Neither did she keep house. My butler hasn't been dusted for years. Anyway, I didn't know she was called Belinda. I suppose she must have had a Christian name, but then there never seemed to be any call for it to be used. She was more of a grunter than a conversationalist. Anyway, what of it? What of anything?"

"She has sought my services as a lawyer," said Marmaduke, patiently. "She claims to have been unfairly dismissed."

"What? She left of her own accord. I still have her resignation letter. I plan to frame it." Grimwood smiled at his own joke. He was rather pleased with the way this conversation was going.

"Mrs. Budd tells me you attacked her using a small boy as a weapon. This resulted in her suffering shock, trauma, a bruised knee and trolley burn."

"Trolley burn? Is that serious?"

"Very serious, Mr... Streep, I assume?"

"Assume all you like."

"I have been instructed to tell you that Mrs. Budd will be very happy to settle out of court."

"She can settle where she likes. Her movements are no longer my concern. As long as she's off my property I am relaxed about where she chooses to settle."

"She will be seeking substantial damages."

"Why would anyone seek damages? If she wants damage, she should eat some of her own mulligatawny soup. I suspect it may have damaged my digestive system beyond repair."

"Mr. Streep, do you understand what I am trying to say to you?"

"I must confess I do not. You fail to communicate effectively."

"Mr Streep, I have never lost a case."

"I'm not surprised. If you managed to lose a big heavy case like the one you're holding I'd have serious doubts about your ability to find your mouth with a pancake. Ah, Molesbury. You have arrived. This gentleman is a Gibbon."

"Indeed, sir?"

"Yes. He's from Gibbon, Gibbon, Gibbon, Gibbon and Gibbon."

"Gibbon, Gibbon, Gibbon and Gibbon," corrected Marmaduke rather tersely.

"Isn't that what I said?" asked Grimwood.

"No. You had a Gibbon too many."

"I say, wouldn't that be disastrous, eh? Too many Gibbons would no doubt spoil the broth. As would too many Mrs Budds. Or even one Mrs Budd. No longer relevant, of course, but I thought I'd mention it. That's what the Gibbon is here about, Molesbury. Claims unfair dismissal or some such tommyrot."

Marmaduke was becoming frustrated with the path the conversation was taking, but before he could reclaim it, Molesbury spoke.

"Are you a minor or a major Gibbon?" he asked. Grimwood looked surprised for a moment, then turned and looked at Marmaduke expectantly.

"Well? Answer the man!"

"I do not understand his question."

"Neither do I. I still feel you could have the decency to answer it though."

"I understand that the firm is a family business," continued Molesbury. "There are four partners called Gibbon, and also some…underlings. Are you a partner, or merely an underling?"

"I am expecting to be a partner by the end of the year," said Marmaduke, his face growing steadily more beetroot in colour.

"Would you like me to fight him, sir?" asked Molesbury, out of the blue. "I was a capable boxer in my youth. I still feel I would have the edge over this... this minor Gibbon who is cluttering up our doorstep. My arms are longer than his." He clenched his fists in an attempted aggressive posture, the strain nearly causing him to fall over.

"Awfully nice of you to offer, Molesbury."

"Thank you, sir."

"Perhaps not yet."

"Are you threatening me with physical violence?" asked Marmaduke, having raised one eyebrow slightly until it resembled a startled caterpillar.

"Well," said Grimwood, looking at Molesbury doubtfully. "I think he's threatening you with something, though violence may be beyond his capabilities."

"I am happy to fight him, sir," said Molesbury, his arms describing a curious arching motion. "He is only a minor Gibbon. An underling."

"Right, if that's the way you want it," said Marmaduke, dropping his briefcase with a resounding thud, "you shall have it. Prepare to suffer." He took off his coat and his suit jacket, revealing a sweat stained shirt that hung off his bony body. Grimwood noticed that there wasn't really all that much to him, and that Molesbury was only marginally the thinner of the two men.

"I say, hang on, no need for all this malarkey," said Grimwood, raising his voice a little. Molesbury moved forward strongly, then began to topple over. Grimwood grabbed him around the waist and held him slightly above the ground, his arms and legs swinging about like an airborne beetle. Marmaduke swung a couple of feeble punches in the butler's direction, but completely failed to connect, or indeed pose any kind of threat whatsoever.

Just then three women appeared from behind Grimwood, all dressed in identical orange tracksuits. It was the three Halanas, all up and dressed at last, and apparently ready for exercise of some sort.

"What is being going on here and so forth?" asked the first Halana with some concern.

"I am thinking that the two old men are starting to have battle, for sure," said another.

"There is going to be some thumping," added the third.

"Molesbury," said Grimwood, avoiding a flying elbow. "Ladies present."

Molesbury immediately stopped waving his arms and became calm enough for Grimwood to place him back onto the ground.

"Good morning, ladies," said Molesbury, as though nothing untoward had happened.

Just then a blurred shape came running into view, arms outstretched, and collided with Marmaduke, knocking him sideways. The lawyer fell clumsily over the briefcase and ended up in a sweaty and untidy heap on the floor.

"Oops!" cried Jimbo, for the blurred shape had now taken on human form. "I've knocked someone over."

"Only a minor Gibbon, young sir," said Molesbury. "There is no need for concern."

The Halanas all laughed together. Two of them moved towards Marmaduke to help him back on to his feet. "I am not being too sure what a minor gibbon is being, but I am knowing that he is fallen over and no longer doing so much of the thumping," said the remaining Halana.

Marmaduke angrily shook off the attentions of the two Dutch women and clambered back onto his feet. Just then, another blur galloped onto the scene, a big red blur that jumped up at Marmaduke and knocked him back over the briefcase and onto the doorstep once more. It then slowed down, revealing itself to be a large red setter, complete with a big lolling tongue and a friendly smile.

"Bluebell!" cried a voice from up the drive. "Bluebell! Behave yourself!" Grimwood recognised the approaching woman as the cook from the village teashop. She reached the dog and attached a lead to its neck, bringing it temporarily under human control.

"Hello," she said. "I was so excited I forget to mention that I'll have Bluebell living with me. She's ever so friendly and well-behaved."

Marmaduke didn't seem to think so. He clambered to his feet, every inch of his bony frame shaking with rage.

"I have now been attacked by a small boy, a large dog, and an elderly butler. I have cuts, bruises, trauma, and quite possibly trolley burn. You will be hearing from my solicitor. Which is me, of course. You will be hearing from me. All of you! You will all be hearing from me. A solicitor." He seemed to be finding it difficult to find the right words, so dark and heavy was his anger. He grabbed his bag, his jacket and his coat, and made his way back down the drive, pausing only to turn round, shake his fist at the group of people gathered on the doorstep, and fall over.

"Lumme jumpers. What a silly man," said Jimbo.

"His sense is not having a humour," said a Halana sadly.

Chapter 7

"Molesbury," said Grimwood, shortly after demolishing a bowl of porridge and strawberry jam. "This new cook. She has a dog."

"I have observed the animal, sir."

"Did we say she could have a dog? Living here? With her? What?"

"I was not in the cafe, sir. I could not possibly comment."

"Of course not. Outside your jurisdiction."

"Yes, sir."

"Lovely porridge," said Grimwood, apparently losing interest in the dog. "It had never occurred to me that breakfast could consist of anything other than mulligatawny soup."

"There are croissants on the way, sir."

"What is a croissant, Molesbury?"

"A sweet French bread, sir."

"French?"

"Yes, sir."

Grimwood looked doubtful.

"A French thing? For breakfast?"

"Yes, sir."

"Do the French eat breakfast?"

"I understand their habits are similar to ours in many respects, sir."

"I suppose so. What were we talking about?"

"The French, sir."

"I mean before that."

"Porridge, sir."

"Even earlier. Back in the mists of time."

"The dog, sir?"

"That's it. The dog. I mean, we now have a small child, a dog, a new cook, three Halanas and a birdwatcher. There's only been the three of us for many years. Now Mrs. Budd has taken leave of the house with a bad case of trolley burn and everything has changed. Is it for the better, sir? Sorry, I mean, Molesbury?"

"Was the porridge not to your satisfaction, sir? I also believe that many years ago you expressed the hope that one day you would see a solicitor being attacked by a dog. That ambition has now been fulfilled, sir."

"So you mean you think it is better?"

"I do, sir. Nonetheless, I will attempt to reach the village to check the veracity of Jimbo's provenance, sir."

"Find out if he's telling the truth, you mean?"

"Yes sir."

"He's not a bad boy is he though, Molesbury? We could grow to dislike him less."

"That is a possibility, sir."

At that point the new cook arrived with a plate of warm croissants and a tub of jam. She gave Grimwood a warm smile, which he almost involuntarily returned.

"Thank you... er... new cook."

"Miss Goodley, sir."

"Miss Goodley. Very goodley. Erm. Good. Nice. You know."

She left, still smiling, and Jimbo appeared, as if attracted by the scent of the jam.

"Wow! What are those!" he asked, staring at the plate.

"Croissants. They're French. Still, can't be helped."

"Crossants?" said Jimbo. "I'll try a crossant. Have they got snails in them?" He sounded excited by the prospect.

"I don't believe so. Have they, Molesbury? No? If you say so. I don't know if they have ants in them though, either cross or relaxed. Best try one and find out. Plenty of jam, just in case. That's the boy. Oh look, you've got it all down your shirt."

"So have you, Grimster," said Jimbo, spitting out croissant crumbs.

"Oh yes, so I have. Disgraceful. I am a pig. Oink oink, eh? Yes. Haha."

*

"Wrrghhhhhhhh!" shouted Mrs. Budd as she slammed the office door behind her, leaving Marmaduke Gibbon sitting quaking in his chair. He took a deep breath, quickly followed by another, trying to use his favourite technique to compose himself. It never worked. He picked up a small ginger-haired gonk he always kept on his desk for psychological succour, and twisted its head horribly.

"I take it that means you don't want to go to court, you horrible old witch," he said, when he was sure she

59

was too far away to hear him. He hurled the gonk across the room, where it knocked an old biro off a shelf. Both items then dropped into a metal waste-paper basket with a dry rattle.

He was not best pleased. The memory of the humiliation he had suffered at Dunnydark was fresh in his mind, and he had been looking forward to facing his tormentors at a tribunal. Mrs Budd's unspoken refusal to take the case any further had robbed him of the potential pleasure. Revenge, however, would be his. He stared out of the window at the concrete, plantless courtyard his office overlooked, and thought about things. He couldn't do anything about wreaking revenge himself. His potential partnership – the goal towards which he had strived for many years – would become an impossible dream if he were to get his hands dirty. He would doubtless stay an 'underling' forever. This thought infuriated him so much that he wished he had kept the red-haired gonk so he could throw it across the room again. After scanning his desk for a few moments he picked up a plastic cup, emptied of its water earlier that morning, and threw it as hard as he could towards the waste basket. The cup described a feeble arc, bent back toward him in midair and landed on the far side of his desk, rocking on its side for a few irritating moments.

"I have it," he said quietly to himself as a moment of inspiration fell upon him. "I know exactly who could help me out here." He picked up the phone from his desk, mopping up a couple of drops of water that the flying cup had spilt onto the handset, and dialled.

Jimbo and Grimwood sat under the shade of a large horse chestnut tree and surveyed the coming day. Jimbo's legs had started swinging back and forth - a sure sign that he was becoming restless with the inactivity - and he was urgently looking around for something to play with. Molesbury stood nearby, attentive and alert, waiting for his services to be required.

"Look!" said Jimbo. "Here come those nice three ladies and that man."

Sure enough, the three Halanas came jogging into view, still wearing bright orange tracksuits. They were followed by the rather forlorn figure of Ulf, in a pair of white shorts and a vest that looked too small for him. He looked extremely tired and his expression seemed to tell of a thousand miseries endured.

"It is the good morning," said a Halana brightly to the three sitting gentlemen. "We have been running the jogging for several times around the house. Soon we will be stopping for doing the other exercises, but it is being so hot, we will be doing them I think very much in the nude."

"What?" said Grimwood, springing to life.

"Wow," said Jimbo, his legs swinging even faster.

"I wouldn't advise it, Miss." said Molesbury gravely. "In England there are laws governing such behaviour. It is not only discouraged, but may lead to a criminal prosecution."

"You meaning I could be ending up in the jail just for the not wearing of the clothes?"

"That is correct, Miss."

"You English people are being so crazy. In Holland land we are always in the nude, and it is fine, and the policemen are laughing and happy."

"I can assure you that is not the case here, Miss. The policemen would be wearing very serious facial expressions, in order to convey severe disapproval."

"Oh, all well," said the first Halana with a shrug. "Ulf will be anyway pleased. He was being so upset that his darling Halana would be without the clothes and having the birds and the hedgehogs seeing her."

"Ah, Halana, you are so crazy!" said another Halana, and laughed, looking piteously at Ulf.

Ulf just looked hot, tired, and generally fed up.

"Come on, everyone!" said Halana, "we must be attending the house for the cold drinks that are refreshing us now."

"If I carry on running like this, I will break a leg or another limb, I'm sure of it. That would be just my luck," said Ulf.

The others ran back towards the house. Ulf watched them go, and then stumbled after them, struggling to keep up.

There was a few moments' silence underneath the horse chestnut tree. Eventually Grimwood spoke.

"Well done, Molesbury," he said in a rather droopy tone. "Very good. Quick thinking. We really didn't want the three Halanas to have… done that, did we? No." There was another pause, during which a solitary male blackbird hopped along the grass in front of them. "Take the rest of the day off," he added eventually.

"Thank you, sir. I endeavour to please, sir," said Molesbury.

*

Marmaduke adjusted his false ginger beard, put on his dark glasses and pulled his deerstalker hat low over his eyes. A few moments later, when he was sure his facial characteristics were completely obscured, he entered the dingy office without knocking, startling a very short, fat gentleman who was sitting with his pudgy legs up on the desk reading a down-market newspaper.

"Who are you?" demanded the short gentleman in a high, reedy voice, dropping the paper on the desk in his alarm.

"I am... well, my name is immaterial. I phoned you. You knew I was coming."

"Did you say your name was ...Emma? Emma Terial? You don't look like an 'Emma.' "

"What are you blathering on...?" Marmaduke sighed deeply. "My name does not matter. You are Eric Nickleby?"

"Who says I am?"

"Known colloquially as 'Evil Eric?'"

"What whattingly?"

"Colloquially?"

"I'm afraid I can't answer that question."

"Afraid I might be an undercover policeman, eh?"

"No. I don't know what that word means."

"Colloquially?"

"That's the one."

Marmaduke sighed. "Are you known locally, that is, by your friends and acquaintances, as Evil Eric?"

"I ain't got no friends."

"Have you any acquaintances?"

"I can't answer that question."

"Why not?"

"I don't know what that word means."

Marmaduke felt his fingers clenching involuntarily. He closed his eyes for a moment.

"I'll come in again," he said and left the office. Once outside, he knocked on the door for a second time.

"Who's there?" asked the reedy voice.

Marmaduke ignored the question and entered the office again. "Hello," he said. "My name is... the lawman. I phoned you with regard to a small matter I needed taking care of. I assume I have the right person? You are Evil Eric?" He said the sentence again to himself, making sure there were no difficult words in there.

"Oh yeah. Evil Eric. That's me. You're the law guy. Emma."

"That is correct. Or as near to correct as makes no difference. The fact that I am a lawman is all you need to know about me. I am connected with the law, but I do not uphold it. I have seen your antics described in the local newspapers, and it seems to me you are a man without scruples."

There was a pause.

"That is, without morals," clarified Marmaduke.

"That's right. No morals. I'm a nasty piece of work. A wrong 'un. Bad to the bone," said Eric, at last seeming to understand what was going on. "A bad man. Really very bad in-deed. Not nice. You wouldn't want to meet me in a dark alley. Come to think of it, you wouldn't want to meet me in a light alley."

"I'd rather meet someone skinnier than yourself in an alley," said Marmaduke with a sneer. "I might be able to squeeze past. Now listen. In my back pocket I have a hundred pounds, which I am prepared to give to you in return for certain favours."

"I'm all ears."

"Yeeees." Marmaduke fought back the sarcastic reply which was forming on his lips. "There are some people living at Dunnydark Hall. A small boy - watch him, he's dangerous - an oldish buffer, an even older buffer, who must be about two hundred years old and who is as crooked as a pickpocket's elbow, and a gaggle of women in orange tracksuits who speak in a strange way. There may also be a dog of sorts on the premises with one careless lady owner, and a youngish gentleman with a foreign accent. I want something rather nasty to happen to them."

"All of them?"

"The boy in particular. And the really old buffer in particular. In fact, all of them in particular."

"That's gonna cost."

"I know. I have already told you I am heavily financed about my person."

"You mean you have the cash?"

"Yes."

"When you say 'rather nasty' do you mean 'very nasty' quite nasty' or a bit nasty'?"

"What difference does it make?"

"My price sheet."

Eric extended a short hairy arm into a drawer and pulled out a sheet of paper which he handed to Marmaduke.

It read:

```
Welcum to Evil Erics

Price guide


theivin - 50              upseting very nasty - 100

hiting - 100              upseting quite nasty - 50

Killing - million         upseting a bit nasty - 25

                          gardening - 10 an hour
```

"Gardening?" said Marmaduke, raising an eyebrow.

"Well, sometimes the evil stuff is a bit slow. I do good lawn edgings. It's my special thing.

"Your speciality, you mean?"

"That's the one."

"I shall bear that in mind if I ever need a lawn edged."

"I would do. I'm the best. Now what do you want?"

"I shall have… is the price for 'upsetting quite nasty' per person or per household?"

"Per person."

"Could I have a price for upsetting the whole household quite nasty?"

"Including the dog?"

"Yes."

"I'll do the whole house quite nasty for a hundred."

"Done."

"Excellent." Marmaduke reached into his pocket and took out his money. "Half now and half when completed. Is that acceptable?"

Eric nodded. "Your beard's slipping, Emma" he said.

"Oh... erm. Yes. Thank you," said Marmaduke, handing over fifty pounds and adjusting the ginger whiskers. "Here's my mobile phone number. Let me know how you get on. Do you have a modus operandi?"

"I can't answer that question."

"No. Of course you can't. What I mean to say is, how do you go about it?"

"I go keep a watch, see what they're up to, see what to do for the best. Or for the worst."

Chapter 8

Lunch had been a splendid affair, and the warm afternoon sunshine was making Grimwood rather sleepy. Seated in a white chair on the patio, the ever-faithful Molesbury standing peacefully by as usual, he began to have pleasant daydreams about the new cook. She was only about ten years younger than himself, and rather pretty. Today she had made a salad complete with something called chicken tikka. Grimwood was unused to such exotica, and he idly wondered if it was the cook's speciality or whether anyone else in the world knew how to make it. He rather fancied it could become popular, given the chance to reach a larger audience. He had finished eating over an hour ago, yet the taste seemed to remain with him, like the aftermath of a pleasant dream. He could make a lot of money, he fancied, if he were to take the recipe out into the world and sell it to the highest bidder.

"Grimmy Grimmy Grimmy!" said a high-pitched voice, intruding harshly into his reverie.

"What? Where? Chicken tikka it's called. Cook made it. What?" mumbled Grimwood sleepily.

"Grimmy! Wake up. Look what I've found!" Jimbo held a croquet mallet and a ball, and was thrusting them towards Grimwood as though they were sacred religious relics. "What are these? It has to be a game of some kind. I've tried kicking the ball but it hurts my foot. You can really make it fly if you hit it with this stick though. Kaboom!"

"Oh, that's a croquet ball. And stick-y thing. Mullet. Mallet, rather. Yes. You need a hoop, though. You hit the mullet through the ball with the hoop, and all kinds of excitement result." His eyes clouded over and a wistful, distant look entered them. "Or used to, in the old days, when we used to play."

"Wow!" said Jimbo. "Croaky! What a strange name for a game. I want to play. What can we use as a hoop, though?"

"Ah. Problem. No hoop, no game. The hoop is central to the action. It is essential."

"May I speak, sir?" enquired Molesbury.

"Yes. Freely, if you wish."

"Thank you, sir. If you'd allow me, sir," said Molesbury. "You will notice that, due to the fact that my extreme age has left me unable to stand fully upright, my body is rather...arched, sir."

"Yes. What of it?"

"Well, sir, it would be very easy for me to lean forward and make myself into a hoop, sir. This would result in a game of croquet becoming a distinct possibility."

Grimwood noticed something for the first time.

"Molesbury? Why are you only wearing your pants?"

"It is rather warm, sir. I am allowing my skin to breathe."

"Aren't you worried about trolley burn?"

"I assume you mean sunburn, sir?"

"Yes, of course, sunburn. Silly of me."

"I feel at my age, sir, the time for taking precautions regarding my health has passed."

"Time to live dangerously, you mean. Ignore your salt intake. Have another piece of cake. That kind of thing. Although cake is purely vegetable, of course, so a rather bad example. You mean it is time to be reckless and have another sugar lump. Oh, hang on, that's vegetable too, isn't it?"

"Exactly, sir. If any of the young ladies currently in the house were to appear I would of course cover myself, for the sake of modesty."

"Of course. Don't want to arouse their womanly passions."

"No, sir. You will also notice that I am still wearing my tie, sir. I do not want to let standards slip."

"Admirable, my dear old manservant."

Jimbo had been desperately trying to break into the conversation. He saw a chance to do so.

"Grimmy, Molesbury said he'll be the hoop! That means we can play croaky!"

"What? Yes, he did. Good old Molesbury. Well, seems a bit odd, but why not? Could you move away from us a bit, Molesbury? Give us a target."

Molesbury began to move away, but progress was slow. "On second thoughts," added Grimwood, "you stay here and we'll go over there, and then play back towards you, kind of thing."

"Whatever you wish, sir."

Jimbo and Grimwood moved across the lawn, Jimbo swinging the stick excitedly. Eventually they turned to look back at the butler, who had gone.

"Where the dickens is he?" asked Grimwood. "He can't have gone far, surely?"

"He's over there, in front of those trees," said Jimbo. "He's putting his shirt and trousers back on."

"Oh yes. There must be a lady present. Look, there's Halana and Elf. Holding hands, what? Young love's dream and all that." The minutes passed, and the gentle breeze caressed the trees as the young lovers walked a little closer. "Right, Molesbury has dressed himself and we've all settled down now," Grimwood said at last. "You first."

Jimbo took a huge swing at the ball and propelled it about thirty yards towards Molesbury, the projectile spending most of its time in the air.

"Wow! What a great game. I like croaky-woaky. Boom!" said Jimbo, letting his emotions get the better of him.

"My turn," said Grimwood. He approached the ball slowly and carefully, checked the wind direction, lowered his head to survey the angle of the lawn, and eventually tapped the ball about two feet. He looked at it for a moment, then nodded his head. "I've still got it," he said with some pride. "After all this time. Some years have escaped me, and possibly my physique is not what it was, but talent lasts forever."

Jimbo waited for Grimwood to amble away from the ball and advanced with the intention of having another whack. The ball landed about three feet from Molesbury, who never flinched. Halana and Ulf were now looking on with interest.

"Ah, good shot, young lad. You've nearly reached Molesbury. My turn. I should manage to find the target from here," said Grimwood confidently. He went through his usual series of procedures before tapping the ball almost, but not quite, underneath his butler.

"Drat. Just too far for me to manage. I suppose I'd better let you have the honour."

Jimbo didn't need asking twice. He sprinted toward the ball like a cheetah and gave it the most almighty hammering, hurling himself onto the ground in the process. The ball flew under Molesbury and smashed into the lower branches of a dense cherry tree, dislodging a large round object from its branches.

"Lumme jumpers!" exclaimed Jimbo. "I've just knocked a fat bird out of that tree."

"So you have," agreed Grimwood. "I wonder if it's another rare one? I've certainly never seen one that fat before. Hope we're not going to be overrun with twitchers again."

"It is not a fat bird," said Ulf, with some concern. "It is a short human."

"Is it? Why would a short human be in one of our trees? Surely that's behaviour more befitting a fat bird."

"I tell you it is a short human. I am not a lucky man or a clever man but I know a short human when one falls out of a tree."

"Well, you're the expert, of course," said Grimwood, bowing to his guest's superior knowledge.

"I am now surely thinking that he has being injured," said Halana with some concern. She and Ulf ran over to the figure that was lying crumpled on the ground. Jimbo soon joined them. Molesbury and Grimwood moved towards the scene of the accident in a more restrained manner.

"What an earth is a human doing in one of our trees?" asked Grimwood.

"I could not say, sir."

"If a chap wants to be in a tree, why doesn't he enter one of his own? I mean, why bother one of ours?"

"I believe not everyone owns a tree, sir," said Molesbury, who had a history of being sympathetic toward the lower orders.

"Really? Some chaps don't have a tree to call their own? It is easy for those of us with more trees than we know what to do with to forget those less fortunate than ourselves. Perhaps we should be gazing upon this poor wretch with pity in our eyes."

"That is possibly the case, sir. You can now clearly see that it is indeed a human, sir, and he seems to have hurt his foot."

"Oh yes. Largish chap. Around the middle, anyway." Halana was holding the stranger's foot and bending it back and forth. The stranger gave little gasps of pain as she did so, indicating that he would really rather she left him alone.

"What, what?" said Grimwood, arriving at the scene. "We have a fellow in distress here, obviously."

"His foot is badly hurting," said Halana. "I am sure his ankle is fracturing."

"Oh dear. Could I just ask this gentleman what he was doing in my tree? With binoculars around his neck, I see?"

Eric thought quickly. He wasn't very good at thinking quickly. His mind was designed for slow thinking.

"I was in the tree," he said in a reedy voice.

"Yes, we know that," said Grimwood, raising an eyebrow.

"You were looking for the Slate-Coloured Junco, no doubt," said Ulf. "Well, it is gone. You are too late. Unless you want to wait for the cat to go to the toilet and then study the results."

Eric didn't have a clue what the man with the foreign accent was talking about, but he decided his best chance was to go with it. "That's right," he said. "You have guessed why I was in the tree. You are right." This answer seemed to relax the small crowd that surrounded him, so he knew he was on the right track.

"So-rry!" said Jimbo. "I hit you with the ball. Sorry you're hurt. Hope it's not too bad. When you fell out of the tree I thought you were a fat bird."

The small boy, thought Eric. The lawman had warned him about the small boy. Dangerous, he had said, and he had been proved correct.

"We must take him into the house," said Ulf. "He will probably die."

"Me and Ulf will carry him," said Halana. "He must be not standing up, and the doctor of medicine must be seeing him. There can be no going for a walk. We are taking him to be laid down in a bed that is extra to needs. Is this alright, Grimster?"

"What? Where? How? Yes. I suppose so."

Halana and Ulf picked up Eric and started to carry him towards the house, followed by Jimbo, Grimwood and Molesbury. Eric decided not to struggle, not least because he thought he might be injured quite badly, and he really did need to lie down and see a doctor. The pain in his ankle was excruciating. As they took him inside he took one last look at the outside world, a lengthy gaze at the beautiful gardens of Dunnydark bathed in glorious sunshine. As he did so, he noticed something that interested him greatly.

"Your lawn edgings need doing," he gasped, but no-one took any notice.

Chapter 9

When Eric had been placed safely in a spare bedroom, Grimwood asked Molesbury to call a doctor.

"There is no need, sir. The new cook is a paramedic."

"Miss Goodley? But I thought the new cook was a cook?"

"She owned a tea shop, as you no doubt recall sir. Cooking is her hobby. Before she opened the teashop she had a career in the medical profession."

"She's a medic?"

"A paramedic, sir."

"What's the difference?"

"I feel I had better not answer that question, sir, as my knowledge on the topic is insufficient."

"Is it the same as the difference between a trooper and a paratrooper?"

"Well, sir, I believe a paratrooper jumps out of aeroplanes using a parachute."

"Is that what a paramedic does?"

"I don't believe so, sir. I suspect she is more likely to have travelled by ambulance or possibly car."

"Though there'd be nothing to stop her jumping out of an aeroplane on her days off, as a leisure activity, I suppose."

"No, sir, though if she has ever jumped out of an aeroplane, she has yet to discuss it with myself, sir."

"I see. So the whole topic of her jumping out of aeroplanes is still shrouded in mystery. We must keep an open mind."

"Quite so, sir."

"Better send her to have a look at this twitcher chap, sir. Sorry, I mean, Molesbury."

"Yes sir."

"I think walking would be her best means of transportation in this case."

"I agree, sir."

A few minutes later, Grimwood entered the spare bedroom with Miss Goodley and eyed the patient thoughtfully.

"Hello," he said after a while.

"Hello," said Eric, suspiciously.

"Hello," said Miss Goodley.

"Hello," said Eric suspiciously.

"Hello hello, what?" said Grimwood, feeling that the conversation needed an injection of vigour.

Eric was silent.

"Hello. This is... Miss Goodley," said Grimwood when he was sure Eric wasn't going to respond. "She's going to have a look at your leg. Ankle. Foot. Whatever it is that's broken. Or not. Sorry you didn't see the bird. Too late, you see. Cat ate it. Flew all the way here from somewhere a long way off, only to end up in Tiddles's tummy. Quite funny, in its way, really. Though not for the bird of course. Or for you."

Eric was silent.

Miss Goodley moved forward and started to inspect Eric's ankle.

"Does this hurt?"

"Yes."

"What about this?"

"Yes."

"And this?"

"Yes."

"Severe ligament damage. You'll have to rest completely for a couple of days at least. Are you able to stay here? Do you have any urgent business elsewhere?"

Eric thought slowly, but well.

"No. I can stay," he piped, the advantages of the situation having finally become apparent to him.

Miss Goodley looked at Grimwood, as though seeking his approval. Grimwood looked crestfallen, but nodded anyway.

"I'll need an ice pack," said Miss Goodley with calm authority.

"I shall take care of it. What's your name?"

"Er... Derek," said Eric, suddenly thinking it prudent to give a false identity.

"Alright Derek, we'll look after you." She left the room, shooting another smile at Grimwood that lifted his spirits rather.

Eric looked at Grimwood suspiciously.

"Right ho," said Grimwood. "No running about or dancing. There's a good chap."

Eric looked at him suspiciously. Grimwood attempted a reassuring smile, then turned and left, only to be replaced a few moments later by Jimbo.

"Hello! It's me. My name's Jimbo. What's your name?"

Eric looked at him suspiciously too. The boy was dangerous.

"Derek," he said after a while, his voice flat and toneless.

"Hello Derek! Sorry about hurting you. Didn't see you in the tree. Thought you were a fat bird when you fell out. Have I already said all this stuff? I can't remember. Gave that ball a bit of a smash though didn't I? Kerbum! If there had been a fat bird in the tree I reckon I would have knocked all its feathers off. I've just run down to the village and bought you a big bag of banananas. They didn't have any grapes. You're supposed to buy grapes for poorly people aren't you? I love grapes. I could eat a mountain of grapes. They had an apple, but it had a worm in it. Still quite tasty though. Not the worm, I didn't eat that. I put it in with the pears so it had something to eat. Are you feeling any better? Miss Goody says you've got to stay here for a bit."

He handed a plastic carrier bag to Eric, who eyed it suspiciously, before putting a hand in and pulling out an enormous bunch of bananas.

"Cost me all my pocket money," said Jimbo, hoping for some thanks from the mysterious in-patient. "Well, some of it. I'll have one if there's any left."

One might not have thought it possible for Eric to do anything else suspiciously, but he managed it. He put his hand in the bag as though half-expecting to find his fingers being attacked by a mouse-trap. Slowly, he pulled out a banana and examined it. Since it didn't seem to be booby-trapped he placed it gently on the bed. Then he reached his hand back into the bag, and touched something hairy that moved.

In an instant he had yanked his arm back into the air, dropping the bag onto the bed. As he did so a huge tarantula fell out of the bag, righted itself, and lifted a leg gingerly into the air. After a quick survey of its surroundings it began walking slowly towards the injured man. Eric shouted, rolled out of bed onto his poorly ankle, screamed with pain and crawled toward the door.

"Wow!" said Jimbo with excitement. "I never knew that was in there." He started to advance towards the creature, but it waved a menacing leg in his direction, and Jimbo thought better of it and moved backward towards the door, tripping over the prostrate figure of Eric as he did so.

The door opened, and a Halana appeared.

"What in devil is happening to make the shouting and the ruckus? There are bananas over all the place." Her eyes alighted on the spider.

She thought for half a second of the best thing to say, settled for "Aaaaaaaaaaaaaaaaaargh," and tried to leave the room at the same time as Eric was grabbing the bottom of the door. This caused her to fall into the room towards the bed, grabbing the blanket as she did so to try and stay upright. Bananas fell everywhere, and the tarantula dropped with a sinister thud onto the floor. It moved quickly along the floor towards the three panicking occupants, who shuffled messily around the other side of the bed, Eric dragging his foot behind him and yelping with discomfort. Now the tarantula was between Jimbo, Halana, Eric and the door, a situation they didn't consider to be ideal.

"Help please! O.S.O!" cried Halana. Jimbo started laughing hysterically.

Grimwood, who had been idly staring out of a nearby window, wondering if birds ever got too hot and started wishing they could take their feathers off, was dimly aware of a commotion in the incapacitated man's room. He wandered over, opened the door, and was greeted by the sight of three faces peering from the other side of the bed, all belonging to people who were waving their arms and shouting. One of them seemed to be Derek, who had apparently made a speedy recovery.

"Up and about already, Derek? Splendid. Not sure hide and seek is the best option though, if you fancy a bit of exercise. You should start more gently. We have a tiddlywinks set in the... Oh! There appears to be a tarantula on the floor. Had you noticed?"

"Of course we have being noticed!" said Halana, briefly irritated by her host. "It is for that reason we are crouching beyond the bed as opposed to standing in the normal fashion!"

"Oh, I see. Sort of scared of the blighter. Keeping your heads down. Very sensible. Where did it come from?"

"I bought Derek a big bag of banananas, and the tranchler jumped out and scared us silly!" said Jimbo, who seemed to be the only one enjoying the situation, apart from the tarantula.

Grimwood weighed up the situation for a few seconds. Then he leaned back out of the door and shouted for Molesbury.

The butler appeared remarkably quickly.

"You have appeared remarkably quickly," said Grimwood, noticing this.

"Yes sir. I started travelling towards the room when I heard a scream. Luckily I was standing not too far away."

"Knee obviously in good form?"

"Yes, sir."

"Well, now that you are here, I advise you to weigh up the situation as quickly as you can. We may need your help."

"I have already assessed the situation, sir. There is no need for the other three occupants of the room to hide behind the bed. They may safely emerge from their hiding place."

"If you are thinking I am to be moving from here there is a joke going on!" said Halana with some force. "There isn't the small chance of a snowball in hell that I will be relocating anywhere that isn't here! Holy moly catamoley! By golly!"

"That reminds me," Grimwood asked his butler thoughtfully. "I meant to ask you some time ago. This saying about a 'snowball in hell'."

"What of it, sir?"

"Well, what I don't understand is what a snowball could possibly be doing in hell? What crime or sin could a snowball commit that could lead it to being sent down below?"

"It is hard to say, sir."

"I mean, what if someone threw it at a vicar? You could hardly blame the snowball for being thrown, though. The thrower would surely have to face the consequences of any action rather than the ball itself. It is merely a pawn in the game."

"Indeed, sir. You have made an interesting theological point. However, I feel now is not the time to pursue such concerns, as there are more pressing matters that need our attention."

"Save it for later, you mean?"

"Exactly, sir."

"Yes! Be saving it for not later but much later! All this gobbledygook about snowballs and vicars when big spiders are scaring me behind beds!" said Halana, her fear leading her to speak rather harshly.

"Miss," said Molesbury calmly. "I assume the spider arrived with the bananas? Yes? Well, I daresay you are worried that it might be a Brazilian Wandering Spider, which is a fast, aggressive and highly poisonous animal.

You need not worry. This is indeed a Tarantula, an altogether more docile beast. Its bite can cause discomfort but nothing more serious. It is slow moving and unlikely to attack unless provoked."

"Can you get rid of it, butler?" said Eric, finally finding his voice.

"Yes. I care not if it is super-friendly and will be kissing me and hugging me, it is still an extreme spider that has been scaring the living pants off me!" said Halana.

Jimbo had ventured out and was approaching the beast with wonder.

"Wow," he said. "Look at its hairy legs! Can I keep it?"

"I would not advise it, young sir. I feel the ladies of the house would not thank you."

"You are very and absolutely so right!" said Halana.

The tarantula, which had been having a well-deserved rest while all this was going on, stretched its legs and moved a few steps closer to the bed, causing Halana to widen her eyes in fear.

"In a way it's a pity it isn't a Brazilian Wandering Spider," said Grimwood. "It might wander back to Brazil of its own accord. So how are we to rid ourselves of the thing, Molesbury?"

"You will have noticed that I have long and baggy trousers on, sir, having dressed after my sojourn in the garden. The tarantula is a nocturnal animal. If I stand nearby it will doubtless seek out the cool darkness of my ankles, sir. I can then walk outside the house and free the animal."

"Why don't you just stamp on it?" asked Eric.

"That would be rather cruel and unjust on the poor chap," said Grimwood, horrified that his guest should have made such a suggestion. "All he did was hide in some bananas. It is not a crime punishable by death."

"Indeed, sir. There is no need for cruelty. The animal shall remain unharmed if you follow my suggestion."

"Well, stand near it then, Molesbury. Put everything into it. Stand as you have never stood before."

Molesbury nodded serenely, then moved towards the spider, the slowness of his gait adding to the tension in the onlookers.

Eventually he reached a spot a foot or so away from the tarantula, which looked at him in a vaguely puzzled way, but made no attempt to escape. Molesbury reached a little way down and lifted the bottom of his trouser leg, revealing a few inches of white and rather wrinkled ankle.

The tarantula eyed up the potential hiding place, but seemed uncertain as to its next move.

It eventually took a couple of steps towards the butler's leg, but then stopped again, as though waiting for something to happen.

Something happened. The tension in the room was broken by the door swinging open and the totally unexpected entrance of Miss Goodley. All eyes turned to look at her as she strode purposefully into the arena, surveyed the scene and passed judgement.

"Ah," she said. "Looks like a tarantula has found its way into the house. Probably in those bananas I would imagine. Good job it isn't a Brazilian Wandering Spider. You wouldn't want one of those up your trouser leg, Molesbury. I know a chap in the village who keeps these beasts as pets. I'll take it around to him now if you like."

With these words she bent over, scooped up the spider on the palm of her hand, gave the ensemble a cheerful smile and left, closing the door behind her.

A general sense of anticlimax pervaded the room. Halana stood up.

"Is nothing dangerous being about the tarantula. Is no need for you scared yellow custard cowards to be in hiding," she said contemptuously to Eric and Jimbo, before readjusting her dress and leaving the room with a slight clearing of the throat.

"No need to stand anymore," said Grimwood to Molesbury. "Though you were doing it very well. I'm sure the little blighter was about to run up your trouser leg. Nearly went up there myself. It seemed so inviting."

"Thank you, sir."

"No need for us to remain here. Remarkable woman, Miss Goodley," said Grimwood to his butler as they left the room, leaving Jimbo and Eric together.

"Wow!" said Jimbo to the inpatient when they were alone. "Fancy a big hairy spider being in the banananas! You would have been better off with the worm. Fun though wasn't it? I might buy you some more banananas and see if there's a scorpion or a snake or something in there. There might even be a bazillion wandering spider. That would be so ace!"

He skipped out of the room, waving his arms about like a big spider and making the kind of noise he imagined giant spiders might make when they were considering taking over the Earth.

Eric watched him leave, and narrowed his eyes. Emma had been right. The boy was dangerous. Very dangerous.

Chapter 10

"It has been another frantic day, Molesbury," said Grimwood. "I must sit in the garden for a while. I seem to have developed a taste for the great out of doors in the last couple of days. It is not as gruesome as I had imagined."

"Doubtless the sunshine and warmth have improved the outside world to such an extent that you are now able to derive some enjoyment from it, sir."

"Quite possibly! There also seems to be more leg room than there is inside. You'd better not go to the village today, Molesbury. Save it for tomorrow. Take the rest of the day off."

"Thank you, sir. I will wait indoors if that is agreeable, sir. I shall be in shouting range if you need me."

"I doubt I will. My appetite for action is sated. I am in need of recuperation. Actually, now I mention it, you couldn't bring me a cup of tea, could you?"

"Certainly, sir."

"Good fellow."

Grimwood sat on a carved rustic bench near the south wall of the house, a willow tree giving him exactly the right amount of shade for comfort.

Miss Goodley appeared, having presumably taken the tarantula to the needy of the village.

"Hello Grimwood," she said brightly. "May I sit next to you?"

"What? Why? Why not?" asked Grimwood, slightly flustered.

"I thought we could have a chat, since you're my new employer. It would be nice to find out something about you."

"Me? What? Oh, erm. Well, I... er... are you sure you have the right man? I just sort of live here, eat food, walk about, that kind of thing."

"I'm sure there's more to you than that."

"Is there? Not that I've noticed. I suppose I may have hidden depths, but no-one's ever discovered them, least of all me."

"Molesbury tells me you are a very kind and generous man."

"Did he say that? Awfully nice of him. Well, he's a rather splendid fellow himself. Gives all to the cause. A one hundred percenter. Not as young as he used to be, of course, but we can't blame him for that. After all, who is?"

"Well, he speaks very highly of you as a man and an employer."

Grimwood rather unexpectedly found himself sitting an inch or two higher in the chair. He was rather enjoying this conversation. "Er... but what about you? Grabbing spiders and diagnosing twitchers and making pie? All very impressive I must say. You seem to be a woman of many talents."

"I've lived a varied life."

There was an awkward silence, broken by the reappearance of Molesbury, struggling with a silver tray on which a cup of tea was sitting cheerfully.

"I'm sorry, sir. If I had known you had company I would have brought two cups."

"Oh, I have to go anyway," said Miss Goodley. "Feed the dog, get ready for dinner. Nice to talk to you, Grimwood. Sorry it couldn't have been for longer."

"Oh, was it nice? Yes. Er. You too. Yes."

Miss Goodley left, and Grimwood watched as she disappeared around the side of the house.

"She has a much wider vocabulary than the previous cook," he said "And much nicer eyes." Molesbury nodded slightly, but said nothing.

*

When he was sure he was completely alone, Eric reached for his mobile phone and dialled the number the lawman had given him.

"Hello?" said an irritable voice in his ear.

"Hello. Is that Emma?"

There was another deep sigh. "This is the lawman. Is that Evil Eric?"

"Yes. They call me Derek though. I was quick thinking. They don't know who I am."

"I see," said Marmaduke slowly, seeing very little. "How's the project going?"

"I'm in one of their beds. Gonna be here a few days. Check things out."

"You mean you've managed to get yourself ensconced in their house already?"

"I can't answer that question."

Marmaduke sighed again. He couldn't remember a time when he had sighed at such frequent intervals.

"You are in the house and keeping them under surveillance... I mean, you are keeping an eye on them?"

"Both eyes. I need to. The boy has already knocked me out of a tree and tried to set a big spider on me."

"Did you say a big spider?"

"Yes. It was in the bananas. The cook looked at my ankle and made me lie down. They didn't have any grapes in the shop."

"Have you been drinking?"

There was a pause. "I had some tea," came the eventual reply.

Marmaduke gave a final sigh. "Well, at least you're in there. Keep up the bad work."

"I'll phone when I've done the nasty thing."

"Excellent. Don't let me down."

"Trust me."

Eric ended the call and gazed out of the window. The view was a very beautiful one, with the sky an azure blue and the trees and lawn a vivid summery green. He bathed in the glory for a few moments, wondering if there wasn't more to life than being evil. Then, sensing someone new had entered the room, he turned around quickly.

"Hullo!" said the stranger brightly. "My name is Halana. I have not been enjoying the pleasure of having met you to now. I have been brought to you by a cup of tea."

Eric looked at her, as though unsure how to reply.

"You are certainly Derek?"

"Eric. No, sorry, Derek."

"You' re surely forgetting your name?"

"Er... yes. No. Tea. Ta."

"It is a lovely view. I am hearing that your leg has been hurting you, and put is what you must be staying."

Eric looked back at the grounds. It was indeed a lovely view. Since Halana seemed friendly, and something had been interesting him, he asked the newcomer a question.

"Why has that tree got a fence round it? Do you know?"

"Which tree are you being seeing? Oh yes. The butler tells me it is meaning so much to Grimbo that nobody, even I think the rabbits and the squirrels, are not to be touching it. I don't know why. I think it is a special tree, for sure, maybe being magic or having the fairies."

She laughed out loud at her own observation. Eric laughed too, surprising himself.

"I will be leaving you now. Remember I am Halana, but all of my friends are too, so it is being fun and confusing."

"Er, yes. Okay. Cheers. Thank you." Eric didn't say 'thank you' very often, and was shocked at himself.

Halana left. Eric, his mind more alive than it usually was, turned toward the fenced tree, which could not have been more than about twenty years old, and thought hard. Then he realised what he had to do to upset these people quite nasty.

He had to cut down that tree.

Chapter 11

After another splendid meal and another superb night's sleep, Grimwood awoke with a peculiar feeling in the pit of his stomach. Something was wrong. He bumbled out of bed, opened the curtains, and looked out at the morning with absolute horror.

"Molesbury!" he yelled. "Molesbury! Come quickly!"

Molesbury, who had been waiting outside the door for his master to rise, entered, and moved as quickly as his bent and ancient frame would allow him.

"What is it, sir? You sound distressed."

"Something has gone wrong with the weather!"

"You mean it is raining, sir?"

"Precisely! Rain! This is supposed to be an idyll, is it not? Perfect summer, never-ending sunshine and the rest of it."

"It is usual for it to rain upon occasion, sir."

"Even on large houses such as this one?"

"Yes, sir. The rain falls on each one of us, independent of means."

"I can't remember it raining for years."

"It has rained on several occasions this year, sir. Remember you were not in the habit of leaving the house until very recently."

"So I may have missed it? It may have rained whilst my back was turned?"

"Precisely, sir. Or you were engaged upon activities of an indoor nature."

"Well, what is the boy going to do all day? Not that I'm interested in his welfare at all. Sooner we get rid of him the better of course. I'm worried he may be under our feet, that's all. Don't wish any harm upon him. Pleasant lad. Just nothing to do with us, as far as we are aware. He should be fully occupied. Idle hands do the devilish things and other whatnot."

"I understand, sir. You need not worry. The boy has risen from his bed and discovered a box of toys beneath the stairway. He is currently investigating the contents thereof."

"Is he showing enthusiasm for said contents?"

"He is quite beside himself with excitement, sir."

"Well, isn't he always? I must breakfast and see what he is up to. Make sure he isn't breaking anything. Still... I suppose...it's nice to see the toys being used. That is what they are for. Is it not?"

"I agree, sir."

"Good."

Jimbo's enthusiasm for the toy box was in fact so obvious that the sounds generated by his pleasant play permeated the house and interrupted the breakfast of the other occupants.

"My words!" a Halana said as she toyed with a fried egg. "It sounds as if there are a group of elephants doing the dancing! I am thinking that someone may be arriving from the hole in the ceiling if they are not to be very careful."

"Elephants, eh? Yes, I suppose it does," Grimwood replied. "Molesbury, set off in the direction of the hubbub. I will join you as soon as this croissant has entered my stomach."

"Certainly, sir."

"This Jimbo," said Grimwood to Ulf and the three Halanas when his butler had removed himself from the room. "What do you think of him?"

"He is certainly making noise with the playing and the having fun, for sure. I like him," replied a Halana.

"He is too lively," said Ulf dolefully. "He disturbs me so. He has his whole life in front of him. He is sure to make a better job of his life than I have of mine, and I am jealous."

"Ah, my poor Ulf is being disturbed by the infant," said a Halana, kissing him on the cheek. "Such a shame it is being in this case."

"Yes, quite," said Grimwood. "Well, Molesbury may have reached the source of the uproar by now. I will leave you to your lovey-doveys. For sure," he added for emphasis and nodded respectfully to his guests.

The scene that greeted him upstairs was one of utter chaos. Pogo sticks, tennis rackets, trains and other paraphernalia for the entertainment of the young and young-at-heart were scattered everywhere. Molesbury stood and regarded Jimbo with a kindly eye, as though awaiting instruction.

"My words," said Grimwood. "Er… I mean 'my word'. Found plenty to occupy yourself, obviously. Plenty to knock fat birds out of trees with there, eh?"

"Hello Grimmy!" said Jimbo, with tremendous energy for one who had not partaken of breakfast. "What a fantastic wow this box is! What's this?"

He held up an old bowling ball, the weight of it causing his arm to swing back and forth like a pendulum.

"Bowling ball. You bowl with it. Knock over things. Bowling things. Skittles. Pens. Or do I mean pins, Molesbury?"

"Pins it is, sir."

"Wow! Can we play?" asked Jimbo.

"Well, it's raining. And, since you have emptied the box, I can say conclusively that there are no skittles therein. There is a dead spider, luckily a small one, but that would be inadequate. It would not suffice. It would not fulfil the criteria a skittle needs to perform its duties with success."

"We could play along the length of the corridor, sir," suggested Molesbury.

"We could. However, that still leaves the skittle problem unaddressed."

"I am happy to act as a pin, sir."

"You, Molesbury? A pin, or skittle?"

"Yes, sir."

"You have already been a croquet hoop this week."

"I remember it vividly, sir."

"Is there any games accessory you cannot become at will?"

"I fear there are many, sir. However, the role of skittle is within my capabilities."

"Won't it hurt? I mean, a bowling ball in the ankles is not recommended by many medical practitioners in this area. And there is your knee, of course."

"If I stand at a great enough distance, sir, I feel the forward thrust of the missile will have diminished to such an extent that any bruising will be minor, and the pain fleeting."

"Do we have a missile as well?"

"I refer to the ball, sir. I used the word 'missile' in a general sense."

"I wish we had a missile!" said Jimbo, adding an explosive sound effect for good measure. "Is there one in the box?" he added, rummaging frantically.

"I fear you are wasting your time, young Jimbo. We must concentrate on what we have, in this case a bowling ball. Perhaps if you were to run down to the other end of the corridor and… oh, he's gone already. Obviously he has the gist. Plenty of energy, what? Always buzzing around. If he wore a black and yellow jumper you might well mistake him for a giant wasp."

"A distinct possibility, sir."

*

Evil Eric could hear voices outside his door. He pulled back his covers, and put his injured foot tentatively onto the floor. It felt a little better. He knew he couldn't stay cooped up in this room for too long - he had evil business to do, and he was hoping to recover as soon as possible.

He would go outside, he decided, find out who the voices belonged to, and maybe attempt to flag down a passing inmate in the hope of obtaining a cup of tea.

He opened the door, took a slow step outside, and was immediately struck by a large heavy object moving at speed. It hit him in the knee, causing him to lose his balance, fall backwards and perform a sort of backward roll along the length of the corridor. He might well have kept rolling for some time had he not struck what felt like a wiry butler, who eventually gave way himself leading to the complete collapse of everyone involved in the melee. The ball, having followed the somersaulting Eric along the corridor in a nonchalant fashion, came to rest somewhere adjacent to his ribcage.

There was a rush of footsteps along the corridor. The first face Eric saw when he dared open his eyes was that of the dratted boy, who was smiling, and seemed to be on the verge of laughter.

"Wow! Knocked you right over, Derek. Sorry about that. Could have been worse, though. Could have been a missile. Kaboom! Poor old Moley's taken one as well. Are you okay, Moley?" There was no reply.

Grimwood arrived and spoke to his prostrate butler in a concerned way.

"Molesbury! Speak to me! You don't have to say anything interesting. Just the first thing that comes into your head."

"I am not seriously injured, sir."

"That's a relief!" No broken bones, eh? No shrapnel wounds? No scarlet fever? No trolley burn?"

"No, sir. I am lightly bruised. I fear I may be slowed down for a day or two, though I hope I will still be able to perform my duties in a satisfactory manner."

"Attaboy! Top butlering, old man."

Eric, who had been listening to these exchanges in a state of pure frustration, decided it was time to enter the conversation himself.

"What about me? I'm the one with the bad leg! What about that boy throwing a ball at me and knocking me over! First he knocks me out of the tree, then he sets a spider on me and now he attacks me with a... bowling ball!" he exclaimed, having identified the object to his immediate right.

"Oh, what? Sorry. Yes, Quite right. Sorry, Derek. Just happened to be in the wrong place at the time that wasn't right. Took one straight in the knee. Dashed unlucky. Can you stand?"

Eric stood, putting the weight on his bad ankle for a moment to test it out.

"I think I'm alright," he said eventually. "No thanks to the boy."

"Must hurt, though," said Grimwood sympathetically. "I took one once there myself playing for the village at cricket. I was only about nineteen at the time. Wasn't a bowling ball, of course. Well, it may have been. My memory of those times is hazy. It was a cricket match, though, I'm sure of it, so I'd say a cricket ball was the most likely culprit. You can't play cricket with a bowling ball, you see. The bounce isn't right, and the risk of injury is too great."

"I'm off back to my room," said Eric with a contemptuous snarl, and hobbled back to the safety of his bed without bothering to discuss the ins and outs of using a bowling ball to play cricket. This disappointed Grimwood, who had been warming to his theme.

When the door had been slammed behind him, Jimbo and Grimwood set about lifting Molesbury to his feet.

"I think Derek's in a bit of a temper," said Jimbo.

"Well, it's raining out," said Grimwood helpfully. "Doesn't put people in the best of moods. Still alright, Molesbury? No temperature? How many fingers am I holding up?"

"Three, sir."

"Am I? Hang on a moment. One, two, three. Yes. Quite right. Full marks. Perhaps we'd better give the bowls a miss for now, though. It seems to me a game fraught with danger, particularly when twitchers pop up from nowhere acting as pins."

Chapter 12

Eric sat in bed with his eyes half-closed and considered his situation. He was trapped in a stranger's house with some kind of ankle injury. At first this had seemed an advantage, as he had accepted an evil job in the house, and the chance to stay there for a few days had seemed an opportunity rather than an irritant. He had, however, reckoned without the boy. Jimbo, he had heard him called. Jimbo. Just the sinister name itself seemed to strike terror into his heart. That the boy was meaning to cause him serious injury seemed to Eric to be beyond doubt. He thought about the spider. He thought about the bowling ball. He thought about being knocked out of the tree, and his heart quivered.

Suddenly the hundred pounds he had been offered seemed trivial. He had to leave. He would phone his friend Bad Malcolm and get picked up.

He took the phone from his pocket, and tried unsuccessfully to make the call. The battery in his phone was flat. He hurled it at the far wall in frustration, knocking a harmless little figurine of a robin from a small rounded table.

There was a knock at the door, and Halana entered.

"Hello Derek. I am being bringing you some food and the drink. I hear you have been sent flying to the ground."

Eric softened. He liked this woman who spoke strangely and kept bringing him things. She seemed to be always smiling.

"Thank you."

"It is a pleasure for sure. Are you still being here for a while?"

"It looks like it."

"You will be here for the Midsummer Night's Dream?"

"What?"

"They are to be the performance of the Midsummer Night's Dream by the lake here the day after tomorrow. We are staying to have a watch, then on our way back to home."

Eric looked bemused.

"You know, it is a play by Shakespeare."

"Ah yes. Shakespeare. I've heard of him," said Eric, who considered himself very knowledgeable about the arts.

"Yes, it should be the excellent fun and leisure for all. Everyone will be there, for sure. How is your leg hurting?"

"Still sore."

"You will be having the relatives and the friends to giving you a lift from here soon?"

"Yes. Not just yet."

"I am pleased."

"Why?"

"Because I am liking you, Derek."

Eric gawped at the woman. He had never had anyone tell him they liked him before, and he didn't know how to react. He was Evil Eric. Being liked wasn't part of his career plan.

"Why?" he asked again.

"I don't know. You are nice. I am leaving you in the peace now. Have fun with the food."

With those words she left, gifting him another big smile. Back on his own again, Eric found his mind even cloudier than usual for a few moments. When it had cleared a little he had an idea. When everyone was at this Midsummer thing he could hobble outside, chop the tree down, and steal off into the night. He was sure he could reach the village, phone Bad Malcolm, get the money from the lawman and never have to go near this madhouse again.

"These Dutch ladies," said Grimwood to Molesbury as he supped on a cup of tea the latter had brought to him on a tray. "They are very lively, aren't they?"

"Yes, sir."

"I'm glad to say they should have returned to their island home before too long."

"Do you not feel their presence has been of benefit to the household, sir?"

"I do not! Same with that boy and the incapacitated twitcher in the spare bedroom. For years this house was an oasis of calm and peace, which has been spectacularly shattered in recent days. There are noises everywhere.

Listen to that Jimbo boy playing upstairs! You would think he was teaching a gang of rhinos how to tap-dance." A terrible thought came upon him. "Molesbury," he said slowly. "Do you like these interlopers?"

"I feel things had grown rather stale, sir. I am pleased a metaphorical breath of fresh air has blown through the house, sir."

Grimwood was silent for a few moments. "Well, I suppose in the short term you are correct, old butler of mine, though I doubt I would have used the word 'metaphorical'. Rather an odd word. Not as good as 'melange'. Still, I cannot help a small fondness for the boy in particular. The new cook is a definite improvement as well. Amazing what a bit of good food does for the engine of the brain. You wait until they have gone, though. You shall breathe more deeply and more freely than ever before. Did you know that Holland has the least interesting stamps in the world?"

"No, sir," said Molesbury calmly, being quite used to his master's occasional mental inconsistency.

"Well they have."

"Perhaps they are more to be pitied than censured for that, sir."

"I disagree entirely. Though it is typical of you to take the charitable viewpoint, if I may say so, Molesbury."

"Thank you, sir."

"However, the fact remains that they have boring stamps. This is a situation they could have remedied some time ago, if they had someone with the fire and enthusiasm necessary on the job. The stamps job, that is."

"Perhaps no-one fitting that description is resident in that particular country, sir."

"I doubt that! The three Dutch ladies who are staying here - Halana, Halana, and... what's the other one called?"

"Halana, sir?"

"That's it. Knew it was a foreign name of some sort. I always have difficulty with foreign names. Where was I?"

"We were discussing the absence or otherwise of people with fire and enthusiasm from Holland, sir."

"That's it. Those three Dutch ladies have plenty of fire, enthusiasm and even some vim."

"Indeed they do, sir."

"So it must simply be a lack of political will. I mean, how difficult is it to make a stamp interesting, Molesbury?"

"Fairly easy, I would have thought, sir."

"Absolutely. All you have to do to make a stamp interesting is to put something interesting on it, is it not? That would be the sensible thing to do."

"I agree, sir."

"We must ask a Halana or two next time we see one."

"Doubtless they will be able to supply you with some information, sir."

"A poor show from the Dutch, Molesbury. I suppose being stuck out there on that island saps their creative energies.

"Holland is in mainland Europe, sir."

"Is it? Are you sure?"

"I am sure, sir. I can request a Halana to confirm my belief if you wish it, sir."

"That won't be necessary. I have never known you to be wrong about anything before. Not that it alters what I was saying about their weakness in the stamp department."

"Perhaps the people of Holland have other strengths, sir, unconnected with stamps."

"The charitable view again, Molesbury. What's that? Can you hear something? Above the din upstairs, I mean?"

"The doorbell is ringing, sir."

"What? Again? This is becoming farcical, Molesbury. We can't even have a civilised discussion about stamps without doorbells ringing out all over the place."

"I shall attend to the matter, sir."

As was becoming usual, Grimwood watched his butler for a few seconds before standing, overtaking the servant with ease, and reaching the front door first.

The face that greeted him was vaguely familiar. He was sure he had seen it before somewhere, but he wasn't sure when. He was suddenly hit by a flash of inspiration.

"Are you the spoon boy? Have you grown up?"

The bony-faced visitor looked bemused. "Er... are you Grimblechops?" he asked, using the only name he had ever heard Grimwood being called. "I'm sure you are. I remember your face. We chatted before, you remember, when the Junco was here. You kindly told me we could have our performance of a Midsummer Night's Dream down by the lake."

"What? When? Oh yes. I did. Coming up on the rails, isn't it?"

"The day after tomorrow."

"Splendid. Have you come to set up the chairs? Boil the kettle for the actors' tea? That kind of thing?"

"No. I'm afraid I have some bad news. We are going to have to cancel the performance."

"Oh. Did you hear that, Molesbury?" The butler, who had just arrived, nodded. "I heard that the performance will have to be cancelled, sir," he said with concern.

"That's the gist of it. Oh well. Not to worry."

"May I ask the gentleman why, sir?"

"Why what, Molesbury?"

"Why the performance will need to be cancelled, sir."

"Certainly you may. Permission granted."

"Thank you, sir."

"Well," said the visitor before Molesbury had a chance to ask, "The lady who was going to be playing Titania, Queen of the Fairies, has had an attack of gout and can't get her fairy shoes on."

"She has furry shoes?" asked Grimwood.

"I believe the gentleman said 'fairy shoes', sir," explained Molesbury. "Gout can, I believe, cause the feet to swell up, making the wearing of any footwear a painful ordeal."

"Well exactly," said the bony-faced man. "And it's too short notice for anyone else to learn the lines. So we're rather scuppered."

"I am willing to play the part if desired," said Molesbury calmly.

Grimwood and the visitor stared at the butler in wonderment.

"I know the lines, sir. I have played Oberon in my youth. I learnt Titania's part as a matter of course."

"What is Oberon? A game of some kind?" asked Grimwood.

"King of the fairies, sir. In a Midsummer Night's Dream. Titania's other half, sir."

The man looked at Grimwood doubtfully. "That's awfully kind of you, but I'm not sure you are quite right... physically for the role."

"You refer of course, to the fact that Titania is a vivacious fairy queen, whereas I am a bent and crooked old man?"

"Well... I hope I don't appear rude, but yes. Yes."

"May I ask your name, sir?"

"Of course. I am Donald Greening."

"Well, Mr. Greening, I am sure you will admit that theatrical make-up and dress can perform miraculous transformations. I also feel that my unusual build may help define the character of Titania as being supernatural in origin."

"You mean you'll look a bit of an oddball?" interjected Grimwood.

"Yes, sir. A certain grotesquerie is, I believe, usual in modern performances of the play."

"Is it? Last time I saw it was a long time ago, and it was all plimsolls and white vests."

"No doubt the post-war years were not ones of plenty, sir. Costumes were kept to a minimum for financial reasons."

"True. They couldn't afford a proper donkey's head for Bottom. They had to use a brown paper bag with hair glued to it."

"Most ingenious, sir, in the circumstances."

"Not that I doubt you or anything, my dear old butler, but can you really remember all those lines?"

"Yes, sir. I can relay the text to you now, sir, if you wish it."

"Not in this weather, old bean. Mr. Greening will be getting wet. He doesn't look well as it is. His face has no colour in the cheeks."

"Perhaps we should invite him in, sir."

"No, no, no, I must be on my way. We will take a chance. We'll do it. It's a very kind offer," said Mr. Greening, who was delighted to have been given a chance to enter the conversation. "You can play Titania. Do you need a rehearsal?"

"No, Mr. Greening. You can rely on me," said Molesbury, with a stately nod.

"Good. Thanks again." Despite his words Mr. Greening seemed even less happy now than he had been when he arrived. As Grimwood had noted, all the colour seemed to have drained out of his face. He was just turning to go when there was a blur and Jimbo appeared, clutching a tennis racket and wearing a boxing glove.

"Is this is the Madsummer Nights man?" he asked. "Can I be Macbeth?"

Mr. Greening gave him a weak smile, looking surprisingly worried for someone who had just been offered a cast-iron Titania at the last moment. "Erm. I must be off. Yes. Very good. Thank you."

He sloped away in the easing rain.

"Those three Hollandy ladies could be the witches!" shouted Jimbo at his disappearing figure.

"Never mind, Grimmychops," he said to Grimwood when there was no response, "I'm sure I'll be given something to do."

"I don't doubt, it, Jimbo. There's always a place for a healthy young man when things need moving, lifting or dropping."

"I'm good at dropping things," Jumbo replied. "And breaking things," he added before wandering off, waving his racket at a damp fly.

"Molesbury," said Grimwood, looking at his butler with admiration and wonderment. "You never fail to surprise me. Are you really going to play this fairy lady? You are? Well take the rest of the day off. Check your lines. Make sure you know when to come in during the song, and where the toilets will be. Very important, that last one."

Molesbury bowed again, and stayed where he was.

Chapter 13

By the next day the weather had come to its senses and once again a golden sun enveloped Dunnydark and its beautiful gardens.

"Today," said Grimwood eyeing the scene through the window from the comfort of his bed, "would be a good day for you to go the village and make that phone call."

Molesbury nodded. "I shall do so as soon as the chance presents itself, sir. Presumably you would like me to wait until after breakfast."

"Of course. No point in disrupting the intake of essential vitamins and minerals. You may need them. Oh yes, and you'd better wait until young Jimbo is fully occupied. Make sure he has his hands full of whatnots and whatderyercallems."

There was a knock at the door. Grimwood pulled his bedclothes up to his neck and eyed the door with suspicion. "Come in!" he said eventually, unsure of whether or not he was doing the right thing.

Three Halanas burst into the room, all in their customary bright orange tracksuits.

"Oh, Grimmychops," said the first. "There is no need to be playing the seek and the hide. We have been seeing the men in the nightshirts before and are unshocked."

"Different culture in Holland I expect," said Grimwood. "You have doubtless never really recovered from the sixties, or had Queen Victoria in charge."

"You are so funny," said another Halana. "We are coming here at the crack of the morning to ask if we can swim in the lake and be cooled down."

"What? The lake? Swim?" The very idea seemed preposterous to Grimwood. "Like a duck?" he asked, hoping for confirmation.

"Yes, very like a duck," said the last Halana.

"I am thinking that Ulf will be showing you the strokes," said the second Halana, and the other two giggled.

"Yes, we will be like four ducks, with Ulf."

"I am not coming if you are taking the Donald," said the first Halana, with mock outrage.

"Michael," said the first Halana.

"Who is Michael?" asked Grimwood.

"No, Halana said taking the Donald, when she meant the Michael, which we were taking out of her because she is in the love with Ulf."

"I see," said Grimwood. "You have cleared things up. Who is Donald, then? One of the ducks?

"Donald is irrelevant, sir. I will explain things to you later, sir," said Molesbury, before anyone else had a chance to speak. "I can see no reason why the three ladies should not swim in the lake. Can you, sir?"

"Did you say Donald was an elephant?" asked Grimwood, who tended not to be at his best first thing in the morning.

"No, sir. I was merely trying to steer the conversation around to the matter at hand. I do not know of any reason why the three ladies may not swim in the lake, sir."

"What? Er... no. I suppose not. We have a strict rule about drowning, though. It generally isn't allowed. We used to have a sign up, didn't we, Molesbury?"

"That was 'No Fishing', sir."

"Oh yes. So I suppose drowning is allowed."

"Yes, sir. Though it is frowned upon."

"Of course. Especially for guests."

"So we can be swimming, yes?" asked a Halana in exasperation.

"Yes. Yes you can," admitted Grimwood. "If you wish, and are able, then you may."

The three Halanas left in an excited throng, shutting the door behind them.

"I do wish people wouldn't have complicated conversations with me before breakfast, Molesbury. My brain takes on a hint of befuddlement," complained Grimwood.

"I did not notice, sir. In my opinion you were as sharp-witted as you always are."

"You did? Thank you, Molesbury. I suppose once we've eaten we should bimble down to the lake and make sure they're not being getting up to any of the drowning."

"I think it advisable, sir."

"Have your breakfast, then go on ahead of me. I'll see you down there. Is it windy? No? Good. You'll be alright then."

When they eventually reached the lake, there was something of a crowd scene in progress. The three Halanas, all in vivid orange one-piece bathing costumes, were splashing about and swimming in one of the clearer parts of the lake. Further along Jimbo was throwing stones at a wooden yacht he had found in the toy box, and Miss Goodley was walking Bluebell along the shore.

"Seems to be the place to be today, what?" Grimwood asked his ever-faithful butler.

"Yes, sir. The lake seems to have an almost magnetic attraction for the guests today. I suppose the hot weather has something to do with it."

"Quite. Your thinking on the matter is sound."

"Morning, Grimwood! Morning, Molesbury!" said Miss Goodley, seeing them and approaching from a southerly direction. "What a wonderful morning. I'm so happy here! I can't believe that just a few days ago I was stuck in that olde tea shoppe."

"We are very pleased to have you with us, Miss Goodley," replied Molesbury with a slight bow.

"Call me Claire. I'm off duty for a couple of hours. Was breakfast okay?"

"Superb, thank you, Miss Goodley," said Grimwood. "Marvellous croissants. No wonder the French are so keen to wave their arms about and shrug their shoulders and suchlike if they eat those every morning."

Claire laughed. "Please call me Claire," she said again.

"Not sure I should, really," said Grimwood. "Seems a bit over-chummy. Rather stick with Miss Goodley if you don't mind."

She smiled prettily at him, and he looked away slightly.

"I think miss should be aware that there is a wasp attempting to land on her back," said Molesbury.

"Is there? Oh, shoo!" She waved a couple of hands at the determined brute, for all the world like a Frenchman who has just had a couple of croissants, letting go of Bluebell as she did so. Revelling in her new found freedom, the dog ran into the water and started swimming towards a Halana, who greeted her with a friendly smile.

"Ah, is the big dog in the water. It is no use to lick me silly I am so wet already," said another Halana as Bluebell tried to clamber upon her as though she was a small island.

Back on dry land, Miss Goodley's life-or-death struggle with the animal kingdom continued unabated.

"The wasp is now in your hair, miss," said Molesbury, as Miss Goodley swatted in vain at the vile beast. "It has left your hair now, miss. It is buzzing around your neck. Allow me."

Molesbury reached out a hand and grabbed the wasp, closing his fingers around the insect so that escape was impossible.

"My word, Molesbury!" said Grimwood with incredulity. "Won't it sting you?"

"No sir. I am afraid I made a terrible error. When I alerted Miss Goodley to the fact that a wasp was attempting to make contact with her, I thought the insect in question was a social wasp, such as Vespula vulgaris or Vespula germanica. After closer inspection I was able to ascertain that the creature is a solitary wasp, probably Mellinus arvensis. Its sting isn't as painful as that of the social wasp, sir. It is attempting to sting me as I speak, sir, and the pain is barely perceptible."

"Wouldn't it be a good idea to let it go, Molesbury?"

"I shall walk a small distance away from Miss Goodley before I do, sir. I would not like the creature to resume its reconnaissance of the lady's neck."

"What do you mean? You don't want it to fly straight back into her hair, sort of thing?"

"Precisely, sir."

"You are terribly clever, Molesbury," said Miss Goodley. "Though I think you'll find that Mellinus arvensis is actually technically a digger wasp, rather than a solitary wasp. The distinction is a subtle but important one."

"Of course, miss. How foolish of me. I will now turn my back and release the insect, using my body as a shield to obscure its view. Hopefully it will return to its former haunts and stop attempting to form a bond with you, miss."

He did so, and Grimwood saw it fly off merrily into the nearest shrubbery. However, he was frowning slightly.

"Rather a lot of Latin in that conversation," he said to Miss Goodley. "It's like living in Italy. Rather difficult for an old buffer like me to keep up."

"Not that old, surely?" said Miss Goodley.

"Hello, be looking!" cried a voice from the water. "The doggy has being swum to the island and is scared to leave, for sure!"

They all looked round. Sure enough, Bluebell, having dragged herself onto a small island in the middle of the lake, was now pacing frantically up and down as though reluctant to get back into the water.

"The waters was being full of deep, and it was difficult for the doggy paddle," explained a Halana from a few feet into the lake. "She reached the island but I am now of the thought that she is a scared hound."

"Is no problem," explained another Halana. "I can be doing the rescue, for sure." She swam powerfully out to the island. Once there, however, various problems manifested themselves. Firstly, Bluebell refused to have anything to do with the newcomer, simply ignoring her and looking pathetically at Miss Goodley, throwing in some slight whimpering noises to add to the effect. Secondly, even if the rescuing committee had been better received, there was no way Halana could have carried the dog, which was almost as big as she was. If she could not persuade the animal to go back into the water, she was stymied.

The small crowd gathering on the lake shore watched as the brave Halana shrugged her shoulders helplessly like a Frenchman, jumped back into the water and began the return journey.

"What's going on!" said Jimbo, losing interest in mounting pirate attacks on the yacht and joining the grown-ups. "Coo! That doggy's stuck on the island! I'll rescue him." Before anyone could stop him - or advise him that he ought to take his shirt and shoes off first - he had dived into the water. He splashed around wildly for a few seconds, appearing to go in all directions at once like a whirligig beetle, then at last developed a swimming style that looked like a hybrid between the butterfly and the backstroke. This brought him around in a beautiful arc, and he washed ashore about ten feet from where Grimwood and the others were standing.

"Doggy," he shouted, looking around him frantically. "Jimbo's here! Dog Rescue Team, Commander Jimbo!" Then he noticed the small crowd of bemused onlookers, realised that he was back pretty much where he started, and collapsed in a fit of giggles onto the floor.

"I suppose the best course of action would be for you to swim out there yourself," said Grimwood to Miss Goodley. "Since Bluebell's your chum she might treat you with less suspicion. Bound to know that you are on her side. Trust, that's the word."

"I can't swim," said Miss Goodley, chewing her lip anxiously as she watched her dog skipping nervously along the island shore.

"You can't swim?" said Grimwood with surprise. "You can identify wasps though."

"Yes."

"That's quite unusual. Most people can swim but are unable to put names to wasps."

"I know."

"You're in the minority."

"Yes. Please tell me, Grimwood, how we're going to rescue Bluebell? I'm beginning to feel quite anxious. She can't stay out there all day. She'll starve."

"We could ask Jimbo. He's already mounted one rescue attempt. Possibly he has another in mind."

"Jimbo was very brave," said Miss Goodley. "But I think maybe Molesbury is a better bet when deep thinking is needed."

*

Evil Eric paused at the front door, then took a few faltering steps out into the warm summer sunshine. The ankle felt better today, no doubt about it. It was good to be outside again. He felt a small thrill of freedom as he meandered onto the lawn to survey the edging. That having been done, he looked at the fenced tree. There seemed nothing remotely special about it, and he was confused as to why it was so important to the residents of Dunnydark. It was certainly a beautiful tree. The sunlight played amongst the leaves, creating a rainbow of greens and yellows that pleased the eye, and the gentlest of breezes caused them to rustle evocatively. For a moment he was lost in a better world than the one he was used to, a world of gentle colour and loveliness and near-silence. Shaking himself out of his dream-like state, he looked around him. All the other trees dotted about the lawns were beautiful as well, but they were not fenced. It was a mystery.

Good planning, he felt, was always the way to succeed in the world of upsetting people, and, turning his attention away from the trees he decided to find out the whereabouts of the lake. After all, he wanted to make sure that the crowds watching this play would not be able to see the tree from where they were. He hobbled around the side of the house, watching out nervously in case the Killer Boy should appear, but no-one came into view apart from a blackbird which pecked at the lawn nearby. Peering through the trees, he spied a silver sheet of shining water. That, he reasoned using his brain power to the full, must be the lake. On an impulse he decided to walk closer. On such a hot morning, and to a man who had spent the last two days in a stuffy bedroom, there seemed something wildly alluring about the cool surface of the lake, with its promise of soothing breezes. Besides, if he was to leave the house after committing the evil deed tomorrow night, he would need to get his ankle back up and running. One thing he had learnt about evil over the years was that it required two functional ankles at the very least.

*

Molesbury did not disappoint.

"I have a plan, sir."

"A plan, you say?"

"Yes, sir."

"Could you elaborate?"

"Yes, sir. You will notice that there is a boat, sir, tied up amongst the rushes at the Eastern side of the lake."

"What of it?"

"We could use it to effect the rescue, sir."

"We couldn't, by Jove!"

"You refer, sir, to the fact that the aforementioned boat has a hole in the bottom."

"Exactly. Boats with holes are rarely used successfully on dog-rescuing operations. A boat without a hole would be the ideal. I fear without such a vessel our plan is doomed."

"If you will allow me to explain, sir. I am happy to sit in such a way that my posterior fills the hole in the boat, sir. I'm sure I would prevent the water entering the boat for long enough for it to reach the island. "

"You mean you are going to use your backside as a plug?"

"That is my intention, sir."

"How will you persuade my Bluebell onto the boat, Molesbury?" asked Miss Goodley. "There isn't enough room for me to come with you in that little boat, even if I thought it was a good idea, which it isn't. You could drown."

"I will not drown, Miss. I am very light these days. I am sure I could float to safety. "

"Miss Goodley is having the fine point," said a Halana, who was drying herself nearby. "The hound is not wanting to move without the mistress being there for the assurances."

"I require some dog biscuits," explained Molesbury. "If they are sprinkled onto me, I'm sure that Bluebell will find her basic urge for nourishment will override her suspicion."

"I have some in the kitchen," said Miss Goodley, her eyes brightening somewhat. "Jimbo! Go and fetch me some dog biscuits. They are under the sink. She loves them. Hurry now!"

"Captain Dog Biscuits! Only I can save the world!"

Jimbo shot off in the direction of the house, delighted to have been given a chance to use up some energy.

"Right," said Grimwood, "let's go and have a look at this boat."

*

When Eric reached the lake, he stood partly hidden by some tall bulrushes so as not to draw attention to himself. To his left, he could see several of the inhabitants of the cursed house standing and looking at an old boat amongst some rushes. He was very pleased to see the boy was not amongst them; doubtless he was away causing mayhem in some other locale. His ankle was throbbing, and he wondered if he had overdone the walking. He noticed a dog on the island in the middle of the lake, and wondered why it was there.

*

Jimbo returned to the lakeside with a packet of dog biscuits held safely in his arms.

"Captain Dog Bisc... oh. Where is everyone?" He looked around. Everyone seemed to have relocated to the rushy area where the boat was. "Captain Dog Biscuit Special Agent Squadron Leader Biggles!" he cried, and belted along the edge of the lake towards the crowd.

However, when he reached a small area of bulrushes, he collided with something very solid and sent it flying into the water. It was that nice twitcher, Derek.

"Aaaaaaaaaaaargh," said Derek, flailing around in the water and creating a massive commotion. "Help!"

Jimbo knew what needed to be done. Dropping the biscuits, he dived into the water and began to pull the struggling twitcher back to the shore. Well, that was the plan; however, due to his rather over-enthusiastic swimming style, he seemed to be making things worse. At least three times he accidentally struck Eric on the head, and at one stage poked him in the eye.

"He's trying to drown me!" screamed Eric. "Help!"

Hearing the commotion a couple of Halanas approached, followed closely by Grimwood.

"Help," cried Eric again, hopeful of more success with the strategy this time round. "I can't swim!"

"Can you identify wasps?" asked Grimwood.

"What? Help! Don't let him drown me!"

"The water is only being a few feet in deep, for sure," said a Halana, between snorts of laughter. "Jimbo, be getting out of the way. I will the day be saving."

She waded in and dragged Eric ashore.

"Of all the... I can't believe... the stupid boy tried to... this... I hate this..this..." Eric, dripping wet and furious, was on the verge of the most vicious, foul-mouthed rant he had ever attempted, but seeing that it was the nice lady who talked strangely and brought him tea who had saved him, he found the words drying on his lips. "I fell in," he found himself saying feebly. "I'm all wet."

"Never be minding, Derek. You never should be walking out here with your ankle poorly. I'll helping you return to the house, and be finding the non-wet clothes to be dressing into, for sure."

"Yes, That'd be nice. Thank you." Eric seemed to be turning into somebody else - someone polite and considerate - and he wasn't sure he liked it. He glared at Jimbo, just to make sure he still had some unpleasantness in him, and was shocked to find the boy just smiled back as though nothing was amiss. Still, he thought, that was nothing to do with his evil glare losing its power. That boy was a powerful enemy who could not be intimidated easily.

"What a nice man," said Jimbo, when Eric was out of earshot. "I knocked him in, then knocked him on the noggin, and he was still nice."

"Yes," agreed Grimwood. "He does seem a bit accident prone, though. Spiders, noggin knocks, bowling balls, hurling himself out of trees and so forth. Still, he seems to come out of it smiling. Is the dog still there? Yes, he seems to be. We'd better be getting back to the boat. Where are the biscuits? There? Okay, off we go."

After a brief explanation of the delay to those present, Grimwood handed over the floor to Molesbury who was able to explain his plan in more detail.

"Doubtless you can see that the boat has a hole which I can adequately fill with my rear end. As previously stated, if Jimbo were to then place the dog biscuits about my person, it would persuade the marooned young lady, as I should call her, to enter the boat. Once aboard, I could transport her back to the safety of the shore." With these words he clambered aboard the boat, which Miss Goodley had hauled onto dry land, and positioned himself so that his back side protruded into the hole, with his head and feet remaining above the level of the boat's brow.

"Me, me, me!" said Jimbo stepping forward excitedly, realising this was the part of the plan in which he was directly involved. He showered vast quantities of dog biscuits onto the butler, who merely indulged him with a benign smile.

"Not so many," urged Grimwood. "Don't want to drown the man in dog biscuits."

"Are you sure about this?" asked Miss Goodley. "I can't help but think this is a disaster waiting to happen."

"I am quite sure, thank you Miss. I'm afraid with old age I have forgotten the correct nautical expression for putting me out to sea, but that is what is now required."

"Is it 'keel-ho?' suggested Grimwood. "Haul-away? Land-ahoy? Roger and out?"

Whilst he was pondering the matter, Miss Goodley and a Halana pushed the little boat out into the water. It floated reasonably well. Molesbury was able to steer the boat gently using an arm that dangled in the water, and before long he was on his way to the island and the patient animal.

"Hark-forrard!" said Grimwood decisively, having decided on the correct term, and the spectators on the bank watched in awe as the brave old servant approached the dog. With an elegant swish of the hand the butler caused the boat to rest upon the muddy bank of the island. Bluebell at first retreated, then became braver, and sniffing all the while, gently placed a paw upon the boat.

"Won't Bluebell's extra weight cause the boat to sink?" asked Miss Goodley. Nobody answered, but she could tell the question she had posed had made the others nervous. Eventually, after what seemed like hours of doggy indecision, Bluebell gingerly manoeuvred herself aboard and started wolfing down the dog biscuits from Molesbury's torso. The butler repeated the hand motion but in reverse, and the boat began its homeward journey.

"Bravo," said Grimwood. "What a butler. Butler of the year."

It wasn't long, however, before the onlookers realised that something was going amiss. It was a Halana who put all of their thoughts into words.

"I am beginning to have thought that the ship is lowering down into the brine with all the hands on deck," she said.

"By Jove, you are correct," said Grimwood. "They are sinking. Do you think they'll reach us before drowning takes place?"

"Rely on me! I am now to be doing some more saving," said another Halana, pushing past the others before hurling herself into the water. She swam out powerfully to the stricken vessel, and started to pull the front of the boat back toward the shore. Grimwood felt Miss Goodley's arm tighten around his.

"I'll help!" said Jimbo, and before anyone could stop him he too had entered the water, and was performing his usual impersonation of a drowning frog. The splashing seemed to excite Bluebell, who leapt off the boat and doggy paddled her way toward the boy. Before long her legs appeared as the water became shallower, and she pulled herself ashore, shaking herself vigorously and giving Grimwood an unsolicited shower as she did so. Jimbo, unaware of the fact that one victim of his rescue mission had been saved, carried on performing underwater somersaults.

"Well done Jimbo!" said Miss Goodley, reassuring the shaking dog with a huge hug. "I think Molesbury's going to be saved as well!"

Halana had managed to haul the boat into shallower waters, and, without the weight of the dog on board, it seemed to be holding up well. Before too long there was a cheer as she emerged from the deep onto dry land.

"Thank you, Halana! Thank you so much! Molesbury! Speak to me!" said Grimwood, looking with concern and admiration at his butler.

"I am well, sir, though you must excuse my bedraggled appearance."

"Quite all right. You do look a bit of a drowned fish though. Can fish drown, Molesbury?"

"Thank you, Molesbury! You're my hero!" said Miss Goodley, before the butler could answer the question his employer had posed.

Bluebell ran over and started to lick soggy dog biscuits off Molesbury's stomach, and everyone laughed. Then they stopped as they realised they had been joined by a stranger, a tall, dark stranger with a commanding manner, wearing a huge overcoat and a wide-brimmed hat.

"I am Oberon," said the stranger in a deep, resounding voice. "I have come to meet my Titania."

Chapter 14

It was Grimwood who spoke first.

"I think you must have the wrong house," he said. "I've never met this person of whom you speak."

"Mr Greening assured me that this was the place. I am led to understand an elderly gentleman will be...is that boy drowning?"

"Which boy?"

"The one in the water who looks like he is drowning," snorted the stranger impatiently.

"Oh, Jimbo! No need for alarm. He always swims like that. It's his preferred style. Anyway, you were saying?" asked Grimwood.

The stranger puffed out his cheeks and narrowed his eyes. "I am led to believe there is an elderly gentleman here who will be my Titania. I am Headley Burrowes. I will be Oberon in tomorrow's performance."

"The man who is to be your Titania for sure is in the boat, it being Molesbury," said a Halana helpfully. "He is here, you are seeing?"

Headley looked into the boat.

"This gentleman here will be Titania?" asked Headley disbelievingly.

"I will, sir," said Molesbury, brushing a stickleback off his shoulder.

"You appear to be covered in wet dog biscuits, which, as we speak, are being licked from your person by a large animal."

"Bluebell," said Miss Goodley.

"You also appear," Headley went on, ignoring her, "to have rising damp, and to have your posterior wedged into a hole in the bottom of a boat."

"All of these things are observable truths, Mr. Burrowes," said Molesbury calmly. "Though I am hopeful that I will soon be able to resume my more usual lifestyle."

Headley sighed. "I must inform you that I, Headley Burrowes, have played opposite Dame Judi, and I expect Titanias of a high standard."

"Who is Dame Judi?" asked Grimwood. Before Headley could answer, something else occurred to him. "Is she a woman?"

"Of course she is a woman!" Headley exploded. "Why on earth shouldn't she be a woman?"

"Well," said Grimwood, "if she is on the stage, I thought she might be a Pantomime Dame, which is usually a chap in a dress, is it not, Molesbury?"

"That is the tradition, sir," said Molesbury helpfully. "Though in this case I believe the Dame Mr. Burrowes is referring to is in fact a lady of some repute in the acting profession, sir."

"I see. And he believes you cannot match her?"

"That is the impression I received, sir."

"Rather a cheek, what?"

"Rather a cheek? Rather a cheek?" exploded Headley. "Do you really think Dame Judi would have allowed herself to be seen in public with her posterior rammed into the bottom of a boat, covered in dog biscuits and playing host to several small fish? She would not. She has too much quality."

"You should be going away now," said a Halana crossly. "You're becoming here without invite and doing rudeness with a good man who has been making the dog rescued, for sure."

"Oh, I am going," said Headley furiously. "But let me tell you this. If you fail to perform tomorrow night, I shall... I shall...........bah!" He shook his fist, turned on his heel and strode back from whence he came, his overcoat flapping like an angry bat.

*

It had been such a warm day that the cool breezes of the evening came as manna from heaven to the tweed-suited Grimwood as he sat on the patio outside the drawing room windows. He waved a friendly hand as Miss Goodley passed by.

"Capital pie tonight, Miss Goodley."

"Thank you, Grimwood. Please call me Claire. Would you care to accompany me on a walk around the grounds?"

"What? A walk? Me?"

Grimwood, being unused to the domestic staff requesting his company on their evening perambulations, was slightly taken aback.

"Yes, a walk," Miss Goodley repeated.

"What do you mean, a walk?"

"I mean we put one foot in front of the other, and continue to do so until we have covered a distance of our choosing."

"Oh yes, I see. That kind of walk. Rightio!"

He rose and joined the cook, and before too long they had reached the scented corridors of the herbaceous borders, in which a few late bees were taking refreshment.

"You have lived here on your own for a long time," said Miss Goodley eventually.

"Yes. I know. Though I did have the former cook, Mrs. Budd, to keep me company. Her vocabulary was rather limited though. Conversation tended to falter. And of course I had Molesbury, my ever-faithful servant."

"That's true. I suppose that helps ease the loneliness. He's a remarkable man. He'll do anything for you, or anyone else."

"Yes. You do sort of get used to it after a while, though. Perhaps I have not appreciated the man as much as I should have done."

"I think you should let him go."

"Why? Is he trapped somewhere? In a snare, perhaps?" asked Grimwood with some alarm.

"No, I mean I think you should let him retire. He's been your loyal servant for so many years, he deserves a break. He could still live here, but as a friend and companion rather than as a butler."

"Yes, I suppose I should," Grimwood said after a while. "I should. I should indeed. But who would look after me? Molesburys don't grow on trees."

"I will."

"You? Be my butler? I mean butleress? Butlerette? Ladybutler?"

"Well, just look after things generally."

Grimwood was silent for a few moments. He felt as though the peaceful herbaceous borders were actually the trenches, and there were bombs going off all around him. Eventually he recovered his composure and a thought occurred to him.

"I don't think Molesbury wants to retire. He lives to serve." He looked Miss Goodley straight in the eye as he spoke but her prettiness unnerved him and he stared at a large bumblebee instead, which he found less threatening. It reminded him of another topic he had been meaning to bring up in conversation.

"Wasps," he said, happy to have changed the subject without too much difficulty. "Wasps. That's what I want to talk about."

"What of them?"

"Well, how come you can identify them? And how come you can do other things, interesting things, like the thing you did earlier, that I can't remember? Jumping out of planes, that's it."

"I've led an interesting life, I'm glad to say. I was once married to an ecologist, and I have been a nurse, and

I've run a couple of businesses. I've never jumped out of a plane, though. I think you may have been misinformed on that point."

"I see. I can't remember who told me that to be honest. Anyway, how come you ended up running around in a tea shop wearing an apron? Not that there's anything wrong in that, of course. Just seems a strange career move for a lady who was once married to an ecothingy. Though I suppose if there was a wasp in the cream cake it would be useful to know if it was a solitary animal, or a social one who intended to invite its friends in to do some digging."

"My husband left the two of us, and we had to get by however we could."

"The two of you?"

"Yes." Miss Goodley seemed slightly flustered for some reason. "Me and... Bluebell. Oh look, we've come round in a little circle and we're nearly home. Well, thank you for the walk, Grimwood. You are a charming companion."

"What? Me?"

"Yes, you."

"Oh. Well, I don't know about that. Seemed a bit of a short walk. Anyway, thank you. I suppose tomorrow we shall be crawling with actors and members of the public and fairies and so forth. Best appreciate the quietness whilst we can."

*

As Molesury prepared the toothpaste and brush for his master, Grimwood spoke to him not as a butler, but as a friend.

"You know, Moley, I have something to say that might shock you."

"Indeed, sir? Do you want me to sit down?"

"Possibly it will be for the best, yes. I don't want you wobbling all over the place. Not at your age."

Molesbury sat down and waited respectfully for the bombshell.

"Today has been... an enjoyable day, Molesbury."

Molesbury rocked slightly but managed to remain seated in an upright position.

"Enjoyable, sir?"

"Yes, Molesbury, and no, I have not been drinking. The dog on the island was... fun."

"Fun, sir?"

"Yes. What is more, I've just enjoyed a pleasant stroll with Miss Goodley."

"Pleasant, sir?"

"Watching Jimbo attempting to swim was rather jolly."

"Jolly, sir?"

"Yes. Jolly is what I said, and jolly is what I meant. Perhaps my strategy of leaving the human race behind me for all these years was... no, I can't say it. I have said enough. Do you feel well enough to stand?"

"I think, so sir. I shall do so slowly. Safety first, sir. I have, after all, just been party to some shocking news."

The loyal fellow stood, composed himself, bowed, and went on his way.

Chapter 15

As predicted, the action and excitement started early the next day, with the arrival of a rather flustered looking Mr. Greening.

"Capital weather," cried out Grimwood upon seeing his visitor. "Molesbury tells me the forecast is tremendous. He has a wireless, and is therefore privy to information such as this. Though why they call the thing a wireless is a mystery, since the back has come off, and there are wires all over the place. It is a positive nest of wires. You couldn't imagine a less wireless item."

"I have Titania's costume," said Mr. Greening, ignoring the topic under discussion and introducing his own. "Do you think your butler could try it on? Perhaps it won't fit, and we'll have to cancel the whole thing." He sounded almost hopeful.

Grimwood took it from him and examined it closely.

"Bit skimpy," he announced. "Might not flatter the poor fellow."

"We'll cross that bridge if and when we come to it. Do you think it will rain?" asked Greening, biting his lip and raising his eyes. "Sometimes the forecast gets it wrong."

"Glorious weather. Not a chance of rain," said Grimwood, who was becoming used to Mr. Greening's frequent changes of subject matter.

"Is the ground flat enough for the seats?" asked Mr. Greening.

"Flattest patch in the county. Never walked upon a flatter patch. Not even an anthill. Hopeless for sledging."

"You still have the dress."

"What dress?"

"The one in your hands! For your butler."

"Yes."

"Perhaps you could give it to him?"

"I will when he arrives. He's still several yards away."

"Could you not move towards him to give him the dress?"

"I could, but it seems a shame to when he's built up so much momentum during his journey."

"You are sure the ground is flat?"

"As a flatworm."

"You are certain it won't rain?"

"I'd bet Molesbury's black boots it won't."

"Is that my dress, sir?" asked Molesbury, who had propelled himself sufficiently forward to enter into the conversation.

"Yes. Best try it on. Not sure it's your colour. You have a pale skin tone. Not sure lilac is you, though there are some darker streaks of crimson on the sleeves."

"They may help the overall effect, sir."

"Please hurry," said Mr. Greening. "Headley will be here soon, and I don't think he's going to be very pleased about things. He's performed with Dame Judi, you know."

"I know," said Grimwood. "He seemed very keen to tell us, as if we would know who this old panto dame is or was."

Molesbury bowed, and took the dress back into the recesses of the house. Jimbo appeared, carrying a toy sword, and ran past Mr. Greening into the garden.

"Once more unto the breeches dear pals!" he yelled, before attacking a privet hedge with undue vigour.

"You may want to do something else. You know, occupy yourself. Moley can be a bit of a slow mover," said Grimwood to the nervously fidgeting Mr. Greening.

Mr Greening turned purple and emitted a noise that was open to a great many interpretations, none of them related to inner happiness. Grimwood, feeling a bit embarrassed and awkward, walked past him and joined Jimbo.

"We'd better occupy ourselves until this strange matter has been sorted to everyone's satisfaction, young Jimbo-chops. Keep out of the way. Devil makes hands for idle workers, you know."

"Grimmy?" asked Jimbo, all wide-eyed, "do you have a car?"

"A car?" said Grimwood, stressing the word 'car' as if he had never heard it before in his life. "A car, my word! Goodness me, no. What would I want a car for? I never go anywhere. A car is the last thing I would need or want. A car, eh? What a question. A car. Me. Preposterous." He stopped and thought for a moment. "Yes, I do have one actually. It's in the garage."

"Wowsa!" said Jimbo. "Can we go and see? I bet it's a big fast one with an engine that could conquer space."

"Yes, of course you can, young man, if that is your heart's desire. I haven't driven it for a long time. It's probably home to several families of woodlice. Or worse! Badgers! Foxes! Bats! Brazilian Wandering Spiders! Could be anything in there."

"That's even better!" said Jimbo, barely able to contain his excitement. "A car full of badgers and bats! Let's hurry, Grimmy! Wheeeeeeeeeeeee!" He sprinted ahead of Grimwood, realised he didn't know which direction he was supposed to be running in, stopped, and fell over.

'Lively fellow,' thought Grimwood to himself. 'Doesn't really need a car. Full of the juice of life.'

*

Evil Eric surveyed the grounds from his bedroom window. The fenced-off tree was there, standing, waiting patiently for his axe to fall.

He didn't have an axe. He would have to find one. He thought as hard as he could, and little ideas drifted across his brain like summer clouds, dissolving as they went.

That nice lady who came in with the tea would be here soon. Perhaps if he was really friendly and nice with her, she would tell him where he might find an axe. That was it! Turn on the charm. She was bound to know where the gardening tools were.

Sure enough, it wasn't long before there was a cheery knock at the door and a Halana appeared holding a tray laden with foodstuffs.

"The good mornings, Derek, I am being here with the fine food for to be helping the tummy be filled."

"Good morning," said Eric slowly and deliberately. There were another few seconds' silence as he tried hard to think of something to say. "You're not from these parts are you?" was the question he settled on, and it pleased him.

"No, you are being the clever to recognise this, as my English I am thinking was much good and so better."

"Where are you from?"

"I am from the Netherlands."

Eric thought again. His brain was starting to sweat. "Like Peter Pan?" he asked.

"Oh Derek, you are being in such good humorous and clever! It is being really a shame that after the day today when I am returning with all my friends, you will not be coming with me."

Eric felt himself blush. He had never blushed before, and he felt alarmed by the sensation. It seemed his body was revolting against him. Pull yourself together, he thought to himself. Enough of the charm. Get straight to the point.

"Do you know where the gardening tools are kept?"

Halana looked at him blankly.

"Please?" he added, trying out his new-found skills in the politeness field.

"You are wanting the spade and the trowel and the dibber and so forth and so on?"

"Yes. And the axe. No, not the axe. I didn't mean that. The others though."

"Why?"

Eric didn't know why, but luckily he had one of his inspirational moments.

"Everyone has been so good to me here, I thought I'd repay them by doing the lawn edgings. I'm very good at lawn edgings. I noticed they needed doing earlier." He blushed again. He decided that when he was free of this prison he would go and see a doctor. Something needed to be done about this defect in his body's responses. He couldn't keep going red all the time when he was around the place being evil. The other criminals might laugh at him.

"Derek," said Halana slowly. "You are the nicest man I have ever been having pleasures to meet. Please have some tea, and there is lashings of toast. I will tell you where you are going to be finding many tools."

*

Grimwood went around the back of the garage, opened the side door and, after much groping, found a light switch.

"The car," he said after a while.

Jimbo appeared in front of Grimwood so quickly, he was sure the youngster must actually have run between his legs.

"It's a funny colour," said Jimbo. "Why hasn't it got any windows?" he added.

"It has a dust sheet over it," explained Grimwood. "The colour you see is dust sheet colour, and not car colour." He found a corner of the said sheet and pulled, revealing an old yellow Bentley convertible in its full glory.

"Wowsa! It's as yellow as a dadofil!" said Jimbo. He peered nervously inside, ready to pull back quickly in case he disturbed a resident badger.

"Yes. Wowsa indeed. Stopped driving it some time ago. Looks rather nice though, doesn't it? All yellow and sparkling. Dust sheet's done its job. Perhaps I should have put one on Molesbury a few years ago before things got out of hand."

"There's a key in the ignition!" yelled Jimbo, clambering over the seats towards the driver's position.

"Is there? Wondered where they were. Well, don't touch them. Not that it will start anyway. Years since it had much to say for itself, I'm afraid. We'll be lucky to get a spark out of it now. The battery will be completely flat. As flat as that place by the lake Mr. Greening was enquiring about earlier. No, seriously Jimbo, don't touch it, there's a good boy."

Jimbo, who had been well brought up, stopped short of turning the key and settled for rocking the steering wheel excitedly in his hands and making engine noises.

"Do you like cars, then, Jimbo?" asked Grimwood rather superfluously. Jimbo just looked at him and smiled. "Did myself when I was your age. Of course, I'm older than you now. Mind you, there's still something about this thing that makes me feel young again." He stood watching Jimbo for a few moments, then made his way around the side of the car and opened the driver's seat. "Budge up little 'un," he declared. "I want a go. And it's my car."

Jimbo shifted into the passenger seat. "Try turning the ignition Uncle Grimbly! You never know!"

"The ignition? What an idea! The car has been sitting - or standing - no, I think sitting is a better word - in this garage since the dawn of time. If I were to turn this key we would hear nothing but a disappointing silence. Listen."

He turned the key. The car purred like a stroked cat and burst into beautiful life.

"It started! Grimbly, this car is a wow!" said Jimbo, barely able to contain himself. "Try moving a bit."

"I don't know if you have noticed, young whippersnapper-me-lad, but the garage doors are closed. Besides, the hand brake will have stiffened up. No, we can just sit here and listen to the sound of a lovely old car having a singsong. That will be enough. I will not attempt to release the hand brake, and I certainly won't press down on the accelerator. That would be a foolish act."

*

Eric's leg was feeling rather better, and he had managed to keep up with the energetic Halana as she showed him the way to the garage.

"These are being the doors, but I am not sure how we are getting in. I am of the thought that there is a big garage for holding the auto here, and a smaller one that is slightly a shed. This is where we will be finding some dibber, and other lawn-edging weaponry."

"Don't worry about getting in," said Eric. "I can get in anywhere. Can you hear something?"

Halana didn't have time to reply. In front of their astonished eyes the garage doors were smashed to smithereens as the Bentley, frustrated by its years of imprisonment, made a desperate, roaring bid for freedom with Grimwood at the wheel.

"Duck!" yelled Halana, jumping out of the way. Eric, wide-eyed and terrified, hurled his body to one side as the car passed by within an inch of him. He turned his head and saw Jimbo looking at him in amazement as the car sped away across the lawn.

"He tried to kill me again!" Eric gasped. "The boy is a maniac! And the older bloke's in on it as well!"

"Brake! Brake! Wheeeeee!" cried Jimbo who wasn't sure if he was in fear of his life or having the time of it.

"Brake! What! Where! How!" Grimwood steered left and right, and the car didn't slow down.

"Look out!" yelled Jimbo. "You'll hit Moley in a dress!"

Sure enough, Molesbury, in full fairy regalia, was standing outside the front of the house. Mr. Greening, who had seen what was happening and decided it wasn't for the best, had dived behind a stone cherub and was hiding his eyes behind his fingers. Grimwood gave a yank on the wheel at the last moment, but instead of taking evasive action, his butler leapt into the car and across Grimwood's lap. He pushed down the foot brake with his hand and the car span round and came to rest a few feet from the side of the house. Molesbury reached across and took the keys from the ignition with his spare hand, then calmly leaned back, opened the car door and disembarked.

"My word, Moley!" cried Grimwood. "You have saved the day! You are a butler who has been known to blow over in a breeze, yet your strength and courage are those of two humans!"

"Adrenalin, sir, doubtless. The human body is capable of astonishing feats during a crisis."

"My goodness! My goodness."

Jimbo was laughing so much he could hardly breathe. Halana rushed up.

"You are nearly knocking through the twitcher and me, and the doors of the garage have been put to splinter. I saw Moley dive in the car! Is everyone well?"

"Oh yes," said Grimwood, his heart still thumping. "Everyone well. Mr Greening looks a bit green though. Perhaps he had a bad egg for breakfast. I feel fine though. Nice to see I've still got the knack of driving. I think I did rather well."

Chapter 16

In the kitchen of Dunnydark, Headley Burrowes inspected Molesbury. He did this by walking around him several times, on one occasion raising his glasses and peering closely at one of the butler's arms as if it were a fish in a fishmonger's window.

"Inadequate," he said eventually in a harsh, bitter tone. "He looks like a very old man in a dress. Titania is queen of the fairies, not queen of the very old men in dresses. Still," he said, raising his eyes to the heavens, "the show must go on."

"Awfully good of you to say that, Headley. We are counting on you." Mr. Greening still looked green, despite having been escorted into the kitchen and injected with hot tea by Miss Goodley.

"Well," said Headley. "I asked myself, what would Dame Judi have done? Would she have glided onto the first omnibus out of town, shaking her head and muttering about Bards turning in graves? No. She would stick it out. The show must go on. Break a leg, as they say."

"I appreciate your vote of confidence, sir," said Molesbury without a hint of irony. "I shall endeavour to live up to your expectations."

"Yeeees. You will have to speak in a louder voice than that, though. Can you boom?"

"Like a bittern, sir?" asked Molesbury gravely.

"Like a what?"

"A bittern," said Grimwood, who until that point had been happy to be a spectator to the proceedings. "Waterbird. Skulks around in reedbeds. Shy fellow. Makes a strange booming noise in the spring to attract a mate. Can't see why that should work, but it does. Actually, the species is quite rare, so maybe it doesn't work that well. Perhaps it should try more conventional methods. Is that the fellow you mean, Moley? When you say 'bittern?' is that the bittern you mean?"

"Quite so, sir. The waterbird you have described is the one to which I was referring."

"What on earth is all this drivel about waterbirds?" enquired Headley in a rather unpleasant tone. "What on earth have waterbirds got to do with anything? I mean can you boom when you are speaking, like an actor! Reach the back rows. Get your point across."

Molesbury lifted his head slightly, despite the fact it clearly didn't want to be lifted, and spoke in a huge baritone voice that made everybody in the room jump backwards slightly.

"ONCE MORE UNTO THE BREACH, DEAR FRIENDS!" he announced. This resounding pronouncement had the effect of bringing Jimbo into the room. The boy shouted the word 'breeches' three times, fell over, stood up again, then returned to whatever location he had started from.

"Well," said Headley, sounding slightly apologetic. "That was alright I suppose. Whatever nonsense you spout, at least they'll hear it. Just don't start chuntering on about bitterns. Leave most of the acting to me, and stand in the shadows. Write some lines on your sleeves, or on your arms. I shall prompt you if necessary. Now, if you'll excuse me, I have to go and encourage some of the younger members of the cast. Not that there are any older members of the cast than yourself, of course." With this, he turned on his heel and left the room.

Mr. Greening looked at Molesbury.

"Without wanting to doubt you," he said after a while. "Are you absolutely sure you can do this? It seems an awful lot of lines to have memorised from years ago, particularly someone else's part."

"Molesbury has never let me down in all the years I have known him," said Grimwood before his butler could answer. " And I have known him a good many years. Isn't that so, Moley?"

"Yes, sir."

"Indeed, he has become more of a friend than a butler. Do you mind me saying that, Moley?"

"Not at all, sir. I regard it as a compliment."

"If Moley says he can do something, he can do it. Though I hope he won't break a leg, as that big chap suggested he might be inclined to."

"Thank you, sir."

"Yes, well, thank you," said Mr. Greening. "I'd better go and make sure the lighting people have arrived." He left, his face still having difficulty returning to its more normal pinkish hue.

Miss Goodley replaced him.

"Mr. Greening looks a bit green," she said. "Even greener than usual. Greening by name and greening by nature. Hey, look what I've done to Bluebell!" The dog had wandered in behind her wearing a shiny, almost luminous crimson coat and a pair of red reindeer antlers left over from Christmas.

"Very nice," said Grimwood. "Er...why?"

"Well, I just thought that with it being a Midsummer Night's Dream, I'd dress her as a big dog fairy or something. Just seemed right, somehow. You do look marvellous in that dress, Molesbury! I'm really looking forward to tonight. Assuming, of course, you won't need me to do any household tasks after dinner."

"Of course not. Join the fun," said Grimwood, just as Jimbo rushed in.

"Wow! Santa reindeer dog!" He immediately offered the branch he had been carrying to Bluebell, who pulled cheerfully at the other end until they were both involved in a tug-of-war. When it was obvious he was losing, Jimbo playfully reached over and grabbed Bluebell's antlers. They both snapped in his hands, sending himself and the dog flying backwards onto the floor. Bluebell gave a small yelp, but stood straight back up, gave everyone a smile to let them know she was alright, and had another chew of the stick.

"Whoops," said Jimbo. Miss Goodley was laughing, and he just looked at her and gave a shy smile before throwing the ends of the antlers into the rubbish bin. "He looks more like a cow now," he observed.

"Or a goat. Ha ha," said Grimwood.

*

Evil Eric watched the comings and goings of the theatre group from his bedroom window in a state of anger and frustration. Not only did he not yet have an axe, but he was also living in fear of a small boy who clearly had murder on his mind. He was a man who was used to the seedier side of life; you didn't get a nickname like 'Evil Eric' without encountering one or two nasty characters along the way. This boy, however, was the greatest of his challenges so far. He had so much energy he was impossible to chase after. He had so much imagination that his next point of attack could never be guessed. Even now, thought Eric, the little fiend could be outside his door, thinking of some new devilish plan to rid the world of poor old Evil Eric once and for all.

This idea made him very nervous. He crept up to the door and tried to look through the keyhole into the corridor outside. 'Wait', he thought, his heart pounding, as he registered a small movement somewhere without. He squinted harder, trying to make sense of the darkness before him.

Suddenly the door flung open, knocking Eric heavily backwards onto the floor. Sure enough, Eric's worst imaginings had come true. It was the dreaded boy. Eric recoiled in horror and tried to clamber behind the bed, but the boy was upon him before he could reach cover. With utter terror, Eric realised the boy was brandishing a weapon.

"Hello Mr Derek the bird twatcher!" said Jimbo cheerfully. "It's a bit hot, so I thought you might like an ice lolly! Look, its one of those pointy ones that looks like a space rocket. It's all different colours and everything. I've already had a bit of a lick of it on the way up, and it's really tasty! You'll have to eat it quickly though, otherwise it'll go all melty and you'll have a big puddle of lolly soup. There was a big man downstairs just now in an overcoat. Lumme jumpers, he must have been hot."

"Get away from me!" said Eric. "Or I'll..."

A Halana came in. Eric breathed a huge sigh of relief.

"Jimbo, there you is at the moment," said the Halana. "There are being some boys and the girls of your same age being here. I am thinking they are the fairies for the play. I was thinking you might be in need of doing the play with them, as inside the house we is all just the truly boring grown-ups dragging you down."

"Wowsa!" said Jimbo, and shot out of the room as though jet propelled, leaving the spaceship ice-lolly lying on its side on the bedside table.

"Hello Mr. Derek," said the Halana. "Nice to be seeing you out of the bed. Jimbo is so being sweet with fetching though the popsicle for your joy. Farewell!" She closed the door behind her.

Eric took a tissue from his pocket and gingerly picked up the ice-lolly, wondering in what way it had been poisoned or otherwise tampered with. When it was at arms length he hurled it as hard as he could out of window, and tried to put the horrendous episode out of his mind.

*

Grimwood and Miss Goodley stood chatting to Molesbury near the front door of the house.

"Molesbury," said Grimwood gravely. "Something is bothering me."

"I am sorry to hear that, sir."

"Your head."

"I'm sorry, sir?"

"Your head is bothering me, Molesbury."

"In what respect is my head failing to give complete satisfaction, sir?"

"Well, firstly, you are dressed up as this fairy queen person, and quite splendid you look too, but you have no fairy hair."

"No fairy hair, sir?"

"No fairy hair, Molesbury."

"You think I should be wearing a hairpiece of some description, sir?"

"I do."

"Grimwood is right," said Miss Goodley. "You haven't got the hair of the fairy folk. I'm surprised Mr. Greening and that pompous man with the hat didn't notice that. We need to find you a wig of some kind."

"Thank you for that observation, miss. It is welcomed. I believe a wig may enhance my characterisation."

"Glad you agree, old fruit," said Grimwood. "There is something else about your head I must mention. Your hair, specifically."

"The fairy hair, sir?"

"No, not the fairy hair, your own hair, such as it is."

"What is it about my hair that is bothering you, sir?"

"There is an ice lolly in it."

"I know, sir."

Miss Goodley took a couple of paces around the butler and inspected the few strands of straggly grey hair that clung on at the rear of his dome. "My word, so there is. How did that get there?"

"I suspect it was thrown from a window, miss."

"Why would anyone throw an ice lolly from a window? Or from anywhere else for that matter?"

"I could not say."

"Whose window did it come from?" asked Grimwood.

"I think it may have been the window of the room occupied by the injured gentleman, sir."

"The twitcher?"

"Yes and no, sir. I have my suspicions that the gentleman who calls himself Derek is not a twitcher, sir."

"He was up a tree, Molesbury, with binoculars. Isn't that typical twitcher behaviour?"

"I have inspected the binoculars he was carrying, sir. They are a very basic and cheap pair, suitable perhaps for horse racing or general activity. They are of insufficient standard for twitching, sir."

"That seems flimsy evidence, Molesbury," said Miss Goodley doubtfully. "He may just be too poor to afford a decent pair. I understand they are very expensive. Watch out, Molesbury, you have a wasp after the lolly. Shoo!"

"What kind of wasp is it Miss Goodley? Solitary?" asked Grimwood.

"Social. A stinger. It's gone now. I've persuaded it to go elsewhere."

Grimwood watched the wasp go, then turned back to Miss Goodley, looking thoughtful. "So, you think the man may be an intruder of some kind?" He scratched his chin. "Do twitchers throw ice lollies out of windows?" he asked eventually. "If they don't, the case against him deepens. In which case, you have to ask yourself what on earth was he doing up a tree with binoculars?"

"Indeed, sir," said Molesbury. "I suggest, sir, that as a minor bird enthusiast yourself, it would be a simple matter to ascertain whether or not the gentleman in question is a twitcher. You have only to engage him in conversation of a bird nature, sir, and see if he displays any expertise."

"Conversation of a bird nature?"

"Yes, sir."

"I'm going to take that car of yours into town to get Molesbury's hair cut and buy him a wig," said Miss Goodley firmly, changing the subject. "You can do it whilst we are away."

Grimwood, who was unused to the domestic staff using his car at will, looked bemused.

"A splendid idea, miss," said Molesbury. "Your plan is an excellent one."

"Can I have the keys then, Grimwood?" asked Miss Goodley. "We'd better move quickly. Remember. Conversations of a bird nature."

"Oh. Right. Okay then. Right you are. Yes indeed. Conversation of a bird nature. Rightio."

*

Grimwood walked into Derek's room without knocking, causing the latter to jump into the air and make a squealing noise that sounded like the kind of thing a pig might emit if somebody stood on its tail.

"What do you want?" squealed Derek. "Why didn't you knock? Is the boy with you?"

The inmate's response baffled Grimwood, and rather put him on the wrong foot as far as starting a conversation went.

"It's my house," he managed eventually. "Didn't feel the need to knock really. Well, not used to people in the house, sort of thing, what? What boy? Jimbo? No. How's things? Foot okay?"

"As well as it needs to be," said Derek defensively. "I can run and I can kick."

"Could be chosen for the English football team then, at least. Some of them can't do either of the things you mentioned, what? Eh?"

It was the first joke Grimwood had attempted for years, and he was disappointed with its reception. Eric merely glowered at him darkly. He was breathing heavily.

"Seen the odd newspaper. The old cook used to take them. Keep myself informed. Kept losing to places like

157

Papua and New Guinea and Luxembourg and teams of pygmies and the French, what?"

There was still no response. Grimwood sat down in the armchair opposite Eric, and decided it was time to introduce the topic of the day.

"Ever seen a Bittern?"

Eric waited a few seconds before he answered.

"A bitten what?"

"Yes, that's right. A Bittern, what?"

Eric tried to work out if he was being threatened or not.

"Boom," said Grimwood, trying to help things along.

"Boom?" said Eric, beginning to feel that there probably was a threat hidden in these strange words.

"Yes. Bittern's boom. Not actually explode, of course. That would be ridiculous. If you attract a mate by exploding then the whole thing becomes farcical. As a twitcher you'll know this. No point in exploding. Once you've exploded, whether or not you have a girlfriend is immaterial. If you exploded now, for instance, you'd no longer be considered a suitable candidate for marriage. Any relationship would be doomed from the start."

"Why would I explode now?" said Eric, his suspicions darkening and deepening. "What have you done? Have you got a bomb? Is this place booby-trapped? I must warn you I can get very nasty. They don't call me Evil Eric for nothing."

Grimwood raised his eyebrows, and Eric panicked.

"They don't call me Evil Eric at all, in fact. They call me Derek. Because that is my name. I'm completely harmless. I won't harm you. You've got me confused with someone else. You've got me confused with Evil Eric, who's come to chop your tree down. I'm not here to chop a tree down. I'm a bird watcher who fell out of a tree, which is still standing. I'll be gone tomorrow." There was a sound outside the door. "Is that the boy? Is he armed? I didn't eat the lolly. I'll bet he poisoned it, didn't he? Well, I didn't eat it. I threw it out the window. Is he in the car? Is he outside in the car?"

Jimbo entered, on foot. With him were three other children in fairy costumes and a taller child who was dressed like an elf. To Eric in his fevered and hysterical state they looked like strange, unearthy beings, assassins from another world.

He screamed and clambered out of the window. The children and Grimwood saw his fingers clinging onto the ledge for a moment before they disappeared, to be replaced only by the sound of two men shouting. Grimwood raced to the window and looked out. Eric and Ulf were both lying on the floor looking rather dazed.

"What ho! What happened?" asked Grimwood.

"I was walking along and a twitcher fell on me," said Ulf sadly. "Just the kind of thing that happens to me all the time. I am a very unlucky person."

Chapter 17

"What do you think, Claire?" Molesbury asked, trying on a large purple afro wig at a local bazaar. "Do you think this gives me sufficient royal fairyness?"

"I think it makes you look more like the king of the fairies than the queen. Grimwood won't recognise you." She thought for a moment. "He really is a dear old thing, isn't he?"

"Grimwood?"

"Yes, He's a sweetie. Do you think he has the faintest idea what we are planning?"

"I'd say not, Claire. He has been hidden away for a long time. He knows little of the ways of the world. Do you not think the green wig may be a little more in keeping with life in the fairy forest?"

"Well, Mr. Greening could use it after you've finished with it. It would match his face. Try it on! The shop won't be closed for a few minutes yet. We may as well enjoy ourselves."

*

The laughter was intense in the garden of Dunnydark, where Jimbo, Puck and the other children had gathered.

"What a weird place you have here," said Puck. "I couldn't believe it when that fat man threw himself out of the window! What was he doing? We don't look that terrifying do we? I thought I looked a bit soppy in this outfit but it was enough to scare the pants off him!"

"I fell out of a window a couple of days ago," said Jimbo. "It was fantastic. People are always falling out of windows or throwing things out of windows here, and a few days ago someone fell out of a tree. It's the best place in the world. If you hang around long enough and you're really lucky someone else might decide to fall from somewhere really high."

"Sorry, Jimbo, we've got another performance in the next town tomorrow night. We'll be moving on straight afterwards. At least we get to stay up late though."

There was a buzz of agreement and happiness amongst the other children.

"You should join in, Jimbo. It would be fun," said Puck.

"What? Join in the play? Me? Lumme jumpers. I'm not in it though. I can't be in a play if I'm not in it. I'll have to keep out of it."

"You can be a fairy. A couple of them don't say anything. They just come on stage a few times dressed funny and prance about a bit. You could do that, I'm sure."

"Yes! I can prance about. I'm a top quality Omylpic prancer."

"You mean Olympic?"

"Yes, that as well. Look. Give me a mark out of ten for prancing."

He pranced a little, then fell over, giggling. The other fairies burst out laughing.

"I'd say nine out of ten until you fell over. Can you frolic?"

"As well as prance?"

"Yes. Not at the same time though. We don't want you to get injured."

"I can do all sorts. I'm Jimbo the wonder boy."

"Excellent. Come on, let's to the woods. I'll find you a few twigs to stick through your hat and a few other things to fairy you up."

*

Grimwood waited outside Eric's room, and when Halana appeared he scurried over to speak to her. He felt rather awkward.

"Halana," he said. "Er... may I call you Halana?"

"What else would you be calling me? It is my name, very much so."

Grimwood thought about this. "I don't know," was his thoughtful response. "Just seemed a bit familiar. Seeing as I don't know you that well." He remembered why he was there. "How is Derek?"

"He is okay. There are the cuttings and the bruise, but he is okay. I am not being an expert like the new lady cook, but I am telling that Ulf has come off the least good, and he is crying in his bed with pain. Halana is looking after him. Not me. The other Halana. I am currently in being the nurse of Derek."

Grimwood shuffled awkwardly. "May I ask... what you are thinking... sorry, I mean what you think... of Derek?"

"Why are you being asking such a question?"

"Well, I was chatting to him about bitterns."

"About what?"

"Bitterns."

"Like once shy?"

"Twice shy."

"What?"

"Once bittern, twice shy."

"Yes."

"No."

"No?"

"No. Not that bittern. A bird bittern. And the conversation became rather strange. Like this one."

"A bird has been bitten? Has Derek been bitten by a bird?"

"Not as far as I know."

"He wouldn't. He is being such a very nice and lovely man. I may ask him to be being my bridegroom and be running away off to Holland with me. He is not being very handsome as I'm sure he would be amongst the first to be admitting, but he is so nice and that is the nice thing that one is meaning everything to me."

"Oh." Grimwood wished Molesbury would hurry up and return. Ever since he had left he hadn't really managed to get a grip on any conversation he had been having. "That's nice," he said eventually, and added a nod. "I'll leave you to it, then. Oh, here's Mr. Greening," he said gratefully as the organiser arrived upon the scene.

"Grimwood," said Mr. Greening, wringing his hands together as though trying to break his own fingers, "where is Molesbury? He seems to have disappeared."

"He's gone to town with the cook to buy a wig. He's there because his hair wasn't fairy enough. Plus, of course, he had an ice lolly in it."

"An ice lolly? In his hair?"

"Yes. Don't suppose it did him any harm. Vegetables are good for the hair. Add body and shine, no doubt."

"What? Well, when will he be back?" Mr Greening was changing colour again. He had become a sort of human chameleon over the last few hours.

"He didn't say. I suppose when he has found the wig of his dreams."

"This is ridiculous! We need him here! What if he is late?"

"Then I suppose the fairies would have to start without him. The wig was essential. He is nearly bald, which wouldn't be right for the role."

"I don't care."

"You don't care about the fairy hair?"

"I do not. We have a make-up lady who could have come up with something."

"You are being so very hot beneath the collar and carried away," said Halana. "I am going off to be finding an axe for my darling Derek. He is worried about there being the fire, and there being no way of him to be escaping, so I am finding the axe so he can be breaking the window through and safely escaping. He has already been out of the window once and out of a tree. He was before being falling out of the window and landing upon Ulf, and the other Halana is beside his bed, and possibly kissing him better." She strode off. Mr Greening emitted a noise like a depressed owl, waved his hands above his head a couple of times and set off down the stairs, leaving Grimwood to enjoy his own company for the foreseeable future.

*

"Well, I think you chose very well, and your new haircut suits you down to the ground," said Miss Goodley, sitting in the driving seat of the Bentley.

"Thank you, Claire."

"We should be back in plenty of time to get ready for tonight's performance as well, even if we give my Auntie a lift. She told me she wants to come and see the show."

"She seemed an absolutely charming lady. We shall be delighted to have her there."

"Off we go, then."

"Yes. Homeward bound."

"Back to the ranch."

"The return journey starts now."

"No point in hanging around here."

"Away we go."

"Chocs away!"

There was an uncomfortable silence.

"The car does not appear to be moving, Claire," said Molesbury eventually.

"No. There's no sound coming from it at all. It's as dead as a dead thing."

"I suppose those years hidden away in the garage have sapped it of some of its vitality."

"I think you're right. This isn't a good thing."

"No, Claire, it is not. Nonetheless, I have a few mechanical skills. I shall take a look under the bonnet if I may. I am sure potential catastrophe can be averted."

*

Jimbo posed before his new friends, showing off his bright red pyjamas onto which some dead leaves had been carefully glued. He had a long branch of ivy trailing from his neck. It looked as if he had stood still for too long and it had grown up his legs. On his head was a stocking cap - a yellow one - he had found in a cupboard, that was so long the bobble on the end reached halfway down his back. His trouser legs were rolled up, and he wore a small pair of blue Wellingtons with no socks.

"What do you think?" he asked. "Will I wow everyone?"

"I think you look an absolute mess," said Puck. "It's perfect! Now, can you prance about without the leaves falling off?"

Jimbo pranced. A few leaves fell off.

"No, you can't. Even better."

Jimbo laughed. "This is the best fun ever! I can't wait to be on the stage in front of everyone, messing about."

"It's a pity we can't get you on stage to liven up a few of the other bits when the grown-ups are talking," said Puck, thoughtfully.

*

Evil Eric sat up in bed, a silly smile on his lips. He was feeling very pleased with himself. His masterstroke of asking the lady who spoke strangely to fetch the axe for him was, he considered, the finest piece of mental gymnastics he had ever performed. He was afraid of fire, he had said. He needed an axe to break the window, he had said. Off she had trotted, eager to help him. She liked him. This was unusual. He was not generally liked. In fact he was not liked at all by anyone, and never had been.

Perhaps, he thought, she was only pretending to like him. The thought caused the silly smile to dissolve slightly. After all, she lived in the house with the boy, and presumably knew him. Maybe they talked together, working out ways to rid the world of Evil Eric once and for all. An image crept into his head, an unwelcome image that featured Halana coming up the stairs with an axe clasped in her hands. Maybe she had tricked him by bringing his drinks and faking concern for his welfare. She could be the boy's henchman, or henchwoman.

The play thing would be starting soon. She would have the house to herself. She would bring the axe back from the shed, open his door, and he would be trapped. Possibly she wouldn't do the deed herself. Maybe she would give the axe straight to the demon boy.

He started to sweat profusely.

Ulf walked gingerly out into the evening air, with Halana linking his arm and supporting him, kindness filling her face as she helped him hobble along the path that surrounded the house.

"I cannot believe I am so unlucky," said Ulf. "I walk along the side of the house and someone falls out of the window and lands on me. Tell me Halana, have you ever heard of that happening to anyone before? It is truly a once in a lifetime experience. I am able to attend Midsummer Night's Dream, though, I am sure of it. I will rest here a while and then gently make my way down to the lake. Mind you, since the butler is playing Titania, I think it will be a disaster. I cannot see anything but failure for the exercise."

"Ulf, you are being such a drippy blanket," said Halana fondly. "I am so sure that all will be swimmingly well good and proper. You are not especially very unlucky, just once someone is falling upon you, that is not the story of an unlucky life! Can you remember which window the twitching man was falling through? Was it that one, in a straight line above you?"

*

Jimbo had run inside to use the lavatory. In the hallway he bumped into Halana, who was carrying an axe.

"Jimbo, you are looking so crazy and fantastic, why is this being very much the crazy look you have gained?"

"I'm going to be a fairy!" said Jimbo. "I get to wear these great clothes and prance about and probably sing and dance and have swordfights and everything too!"

"Ah, to be young is to be fantastic!" said Halana.

Mr Greening appeared. He looked at Jimbo as though he was looking at a caterpillar on his salad, and addressed Halana.

"I don't suppose we could borrow you a moment could we please? If you aren't too busy chopping wood or whatever you're doing. We need someone to help put some chairs out."

Halana looked doubtful. "Oh, but I was taking this to Derek, but... Jimbo, could you please be taking this chopper to Derek for me, then I can be indeed helping this man."

"Wow!" said Jimbo, taking hold of the axe. His eyes lit up like fireflies.

"You must be absolutely promise me to be so careful, though," said Halana sharply. "It is not a game or hobby! This is a serious tool for chopping and you must be walking and holding with the great care, yes?"

"Yes," said Jimbo, putting on his most serious face.

"Okay, mister, show me chairs and I will be arranging of them," said Halana, and walked off.

*

Evil Eric watched the door to his room. His thoughts, that just a few moments ago were pleasant and self-congratulatory, had turned into hideous demons that haunted his brain. He leapt off the bed and made a dash for the door, but he was too late.

The boy was there. He was dressed in a manner so bizarre and terrifying that his mere appearance sent cold shivers down Eric's tingling spine. He held an axe, and his eyes shone with a deadly light.

"I've got something for you, Derek," said the boy. "It is not a game. This is serious."

"No!" said Eric. "Noooooooooooooo!" He turned and fled, scrambling his way awkwardly onto the window ledge and, with one last look at the Boy Horror, fell to the grounds below.

Thirty minutes later, Ulf was sitting up in bed with Halana holding his hand and looking into his eyes with pity and concern.

"Now do you believe I am unlucky?" he asked. "Most people don't have a single twitcher falling on them in the course of a lifetime. I have had two, and I think if I try to go and see the play, I may have a third!"

Chapter 18

Headley Burrowes, as was his wont, had put himself into costume early, and was strutting around the backstage area practising his kingly facial expressions. Mr Greening, whose face was now the colour of a Cornish sunset, walked in.

"Ah, Greening," said Headley, giving every syllable the full weight. "We seem to be short of a butler. The approximately one thousand-year old butler of uncertain provenance who you - yes, you - decided would be suitable for the role of Titania, Queen of the Fairies."

"I'm sure he'll turn up, Headley," said Mr. Greening pathetically. "He went into town to find a wig. He didn't realise we have a perfectly good selection to choose from."

"Well why should he, Greening?" asked Headley, adjusting a fairy stocking. "He is not a man of the stage. He is a carrier of tea trays. If you were in urgent need of a piece of carrot cake, he would no doubt be the man you would consult. However, theatrical costumery will doubtless be outside his field of experience. His knowledge of such matters will be rudimentary at best. The big question is, what do we do now? We have all other members of the cast present and correct, we have the lights, we have the script memorised, the stage is set, the tickets are sold, but we have no Titania! The punters are currently opening picnic baskets upon the lawn expecting to be royally entertained. We shall have to disappoint them. Let us hope they have at least brought their own carrot cake, as none will be forthcoming from Mr. Molesbury, the amazing vanishing butler."

"Mr Streep has kindly given me the evening off, sir. I will not be expected to perform my usual duties around the house."

Mr. Greening looked up and gasped. Headley's eyes widened and his mouth flopped open like that of a surprised goldfish. Molesbury stood before them, resplendent in a vivid green wig that clashed completely with his dress. There were oil stains on his person, one on his face giving the impression that he had grown a rather stylish moustache during his absence.

"What on earth is he wearing?" demanded Headley, "and why the Errol Flynn moustache?"

"I had a slight problem with the motor car, sir. I fear I may have the odd streak of oil about my person. The moustachioed effect is not vanity, sir, I assure you."

"He is here, Headley! We must be thankful!" said Mr. Greening, slowly changing colour. He looked like he wanted to kiss Molesbury but was fighting the urge, not least because he was worried he might end up looking like Errol Flynn too.

Headley seemed less impressed. "You know the lines, do you, butler?" he snorted.

"I do, sir."

"You'd better! Someone like myself, who has shared a stage with Dame Judi, will not take kindly to finding himself working with a line-fluffing butler."

"Leave him alone, Headley," said the actor playing Bottom, who had just walked in. "And if you're going to threaten the other members of the cast, don't do it in those clothes. We can't take you seriously."

Headley looked fiercely at his fellow actor, who was as tall and as broad as he was, gave one last glare at Molesbury, then harrumphed and strode off to a quiet area to practise his booming.

"Welcome to the cast," said Bottom. "Thanks for filling in. Hope it goes alright for you."

"Thank you, sir."

"Why were you late again?" asked Mr. Greening. "Did you say something about a car?"

"Yes, sir. I'm afraid the motor car broke down. I was luckily able to fix the fault, and we still had time to pick up Miss Goodley's aunt, who was keen to see the show."

"Well, yes, alright, well you're here now. That's all that matters."

*

Grimwood wandered in his customarily leisurely fashion towards the lake. There were already plenty of cars parked on the rougher patches of the lawn, and he could see several groups of people with cloths laid out on the grass, enjoying boiled eggs, strawberries and thermos flasks full of soup and tea. How different this experience, he thought, from the years of isolation he had spent within the confines of the hall! He had resisted the world with all his might, but now it had breached the barriers he had erected, he wondered if it was really all that bad. The people who had come to see the play seemed, from this distance at least, pleasant sorts. They brought the place to life, as the twitchers had done. All down to the boy, he thought. That was a lesson for life. Things could go peacefully, serenely, uneventfully, and then a boy arrives and chaos ensues. He could have reminded Molesbury to make the phone call whilst he was in town buying a wig, yet he had not done so. After all, it was only for the school holidays, and Jimbo seemed so happy here. It would have been wrong to send the young whippersnapper on his way, even if he was here under false pretences.

Miss Goodley saw him and waved. She had an older lady with her. They both made their way over to Grimwood, wearing smiles as big as balloons.

"Isn't it exciting?" said Miss Goodley. "The sense of anticipation. A good weather forecast and everyone looking forward to the fun. On, Grimwood, this is my aunt, my aunt, this is Grimwood."

"Hello, auntie," said Grimwood.

"Hello Grimwood! I've heard so much about you. You have a wonderful house. So nice of you to host the show at such short notice. I'm sure everyone is very grateful."

"What? Yes. Well. Glad to help." Grimwood bowed slightly, although he wasn't sure why.

Miss Goodley's aunt smiled, and, linking her niece's arm, went on her way. Grimwood, alone again, soaked up the early evening air, and wondered if anyone had a boiled egg or two going spare.

A man in an orange jacket stopped him.

"Are you here for the Dream, mate?" he asked, in a rough but friendly manner.

"The Dream? What Dream?"

"Midsummer one, mate."

"Oh yes! Of course. Yes, I suppose I am. What of it?"

"Can I see your ticket please, mate?"

Grimwood thought hard. "You mean my entrance ticket? Ticket to get in? Seat ticket? That kind of thing?"

"Yes, mate." The man smiled, as though uncertain whether or not this strange, wandering gentleman was pulling his leg.

"Well, I don't have one. It's my house, you see. I am Grimwood Streep Esquire, proprietor."

The man smiled again, uncertain how to proceed. He looked around, as though expecting to see the guardian angel of ticket checkers standing behind him with his wings open and a word of friendly advice on his lips. Seeing no-one, he looked back at Grimwood, his eyes searching for clues. Surely this rather untidy, bemused looking gentleman couldn't be the owner of Dunnydark?

Jimbo appeared, grabbed Grimwood's arms and swung him around one-hundred and eighty degrees.

"Uncle Grimmyboots!" he yelled."Look! I'm dressed as a fairy and I'm going on the stage. Pluck said it was okay. I'm going to be a film star! Wheeeeeeeeeeeeeee!

Want to see me do the prance dance? I've been prancising practing all day! I mean I've been practising the dance prance."

The man in the orange jacket lifted his eyebrows. "Uncle Grimmyboots, eh? Rightio. I'll say you're a relative of the cast if anyone asks. Enjoy the play, mate." Glad to have an opportunity to be somewhere else, he wandered off in search of more hapless victims.

"You're in the show, are you, Jimbo?" asked Grimwood, equally delighted to have got rid of the bright-jacketed nuisance. "Well, that's splendid. Any lines?"

"I might make a few up."

"Splendid. Don't mention bitterns though. It never goes down well, in my experience."

"I won't, Uncle Grimster, I promise. What's a bittern?"

"A bird that booms in reeds."

"Coo."

"No, that's a dove."

"Oooo."

"That's an owl."

"What is?"

Grimwood sensed yet another bittern related conversation going astray and decided to change the subject.

"Hadn't you better run off and start rehearsing? Play must start quite soon. Darkness is falling. I can see people packing up their picnics. I was hoping for a boiled egg, but I daresay they've all been consumed by now. Gave

Miss Goodley the night off, you see. I'm so hungry I'd even eat mulligatawny soup."

"Wowsa, that is hungry. Anyway, you're right, Grimmychops. Play starts soon." He made as if to leave, then unexpectedly turned. His face looked a little more serious than Grimwood had ever seen it before. "Uncle Grimwood?" he said, slowly, even hesitantly. "Thank you for letting me stay here. I'm having a fantastic time."

"Yes," said Grimwood. Then, two words came out of his mouth and surprised him. "Me too," he said.

"Hooray! I'm off then," said Jimbo, his face returning to its usual expression of careless boyish glee. "Superfairy wheeeeeeeeeeeeeeeeeeeeeeeeeeeeeeeeeeeeeeeeeeeeeeh!" he screeched and disappeared into the crowd.

Three Halanas appeared.

"Mister Grimmychops," said one. "My other Halanas are both having the sadness."

"I am having to leave my Ulf because he is too not well to be watching. Miss Goodley has given him her dog to be doing the after looking, so he has the dog company but not me," said a Halana.

"I am leaving the lovely Derek because he is also having the poorly. I was thinking that he is well enough to come but he is many times falling from the window and insists he is not becoming one of the audience."

"I see," said Grimwood sympathetically. "Well, if you have to care for the casualties, you have to care for them. There is no getting away from it. Anyway, I suppose it will soon be time for us to become one of the audience. Or four of the audience, technically speaking, what?"

He smiled. Only one Halana smiled back.

Miss Goodley reappeared with her aunt.

"Hi Halana, is Ulf any better? I'm grateful that he's looking after Bluebell," she asked.

Halana finally cracked. "I have to be with my Ulf. I will be absent for the show. My Ulf is very much needing me plenty so much!" She held her hands up to her face, and hurried back toward the house.

"I would be joining my Derek and missing also the show, but no! He is so insisting, he says you go! I am wanting to be on his own so much, for sure," said another Halana.

"Plenty of drama here even before the show starts," said Miss Goodley. "Come on, whoever's coming. Let's find some seats."

They settled down. The temperature was perfect. Grimwood watched the sky become paler toward the horizon and observed dark clouds sailing low across the heavens like mighty ships carrying away the last of the day. Then he concentrated on the stage, and waited for the actors to appear.

Chapter 19

"Now, fair Hyppolyta, our nuptial hour draws on apace," declaimed Theseus and the play was underway. Grimwood settled down and tried to enjoy it, but a faint nervousness gnawed at his stomach. Molesbury was, if not physically a giant, certainly a giant in every other respect; still, he wondered if the noble fellow had overstretched himself on this occasion. The actors on stage seemed to have memorised an awful lot of words, several of which seemed to be passing through his head before his brain had the chance to seize and understand them. Surely, a gentleman of Molesbury's age could not cast himself back through the years and remember all he was required to say, and in the right order, all the time burdened by having to wear a green wig? After pondering on these matters for a few minutes, Grimwood realised that his attention had wandered from the action upon the stage. It was the following exchange that grabbed his attention and placed him back in the here and now.

Bottom: A very good piece of work indeed, and a merry. Now, good Peter Quince, call forth your actors by the scroll. Masters, spread yourselves.

Quince: Answer as I call you. Nick Bottom, the weaver?

Fairy: Eye of newt and toad of frog!

Bottom: Er… what? Yes… ready. Name what part I am for, and proceed.

Surely, Grimwood thought, the fairies were not yet caught up in the plot? Yet there one was, resplendent in typical fairy garb of pyjamas and wellingtons, taking his fair share of the limelight. It was Jimbo. No sooner had Grimwood identified his great nephew than an arm appeared from the scenery at the back of the stage and grabbed the boy, removing him summarily from the action. Grimwood frowned, but as he did so he realised that nobody else was frowning. Indeed, Jimbo's unexpected contribution had clearly been a big hit. There was even a ripple of applause. He turned to look at Miss Goodley, whose facial expression was hard to gauge. Her aunt's expression was easier to read. It was pure, unadulterated happiness.

*

Before long it was time for the entry of Puck and the fairies. Jimbo, having presumably managed to wriggle his way out of Headley's grasp, was amongst their number. Thankfully, this time he decided to keep quiet and concentrate on his prancing, and, Grimwood had to admit, he pranced well. All of the hard work he had put into perfecting his technique had clearly paid off. He caught the eye. The only danger was that the dialogue between Puck and a fairy was in danger of being overshadowed by the prancing work being undertaken elsewhere. Stagehands had set up a wind machine in the wings, presumably to help create a supernatural atmosphere, and the leaves that were constantly falling off Jimbo eddied up and surrounded the other players. The effect was rather magical, Grimwood thought.

It was time for the big moment. Headley entered, looking suitably majestic, and boomed out his opening line. Behind him came Molesbury, looking ridiculous but respectful.

"Ill met by moonlight, proud Titania!"

Then disaster struck. Molesbury had edged forward and was now directly in the path of the wind machine. This unexpected force had the effect of causing the worthy butler to topple gently over until he was completely horizontal, his voluminous wig thankfully preventing him from banging his head on the stage. However, this small setback was not enough to deter the great man.

"What, Jealous Oberon, sir? Fairies, skip hence. I have forsworn his bed and company." He spoke well, especially so for a horizontal butler, and the play continued. Headley, to his credit, was not shaken, but carried on booming like an amorous bittern who had heard rumours of an unmarried lady bittern in a neighbouring reedbed.

Molesbury went on. At the words 'playing on pipes of corn' Jimbo had an improvisational inspiration, and ran over to Molesbury and hauled him back into an upright position. He then made the mistake of leaving the butler to his own devices, and the Queen of the Fairies immediately toppled again, this time being captured mid-swoon by a passing child.

"To Theseus must be wedded, sir. And you come to give their bed joy and prosperity, sir," said Molesbury as Jimbo and the other good samaritan fairy hauled him back onto his feet.

It was going well. The audience was in hysterics. They had been expecting a fun evening at the open air theatre but this was clearly surpassing all of their comedic expectations.

Molesbury went on, propped up by the other members of the cast, apparently word perfect. At one stage, though, Grimwood thought he heard him say the words "as from the sea they have sucked up contagious frogs," which he was sure wasn't quite right.

When the time came for Molesbury to leave the stage there was a spontaneous outbreak of applause from the crowd, particularly when a scruffily dressed stagehand had to come and help the fairies transport him into the wings. At the conclusion of the scene, when all the fairies went back to wherever fairies went when they weren't needed for dramatic purposes, Jimbo was still prancing wildly on the stage, spraying leaves everywhere. If he hadn't been grabbed by the scruff of the neck by Headley as he himself exited, he would still have been present in the next scene, which wasn't Shakespeare's intention.

Jimbo had one last prancing opportunity before the interval, in which he provided some piquant harmonies to accompany the fairy song. Grimwood idly wondered if had studied modern classical composition at some stage, as there was some resemblance between the sounds emanating from his great-nephew and those he had heard in a concert of works by some avant-garde composer some years ago. After a while he decided the boy probably wasn't old enough to have done so.

Someone - probably that sensible chameleon Mr. Greening - had decided to turn off the wind machine, and Molesbury's balance was much improved as a result. He sailed through the last part of the first half, his only apparent difficulty being that his wig was starting to slip. Molesbury did not have good posture, and the wig frequently found itself a victim of gravity, and was rescued only by the attentions of various fairy folk.

The interval arrived, and the applause was tumultuous, particularly when Jimbo reappeared on the stage, pranced, sung a few bars of the witches' song from Macbeth and fell over.

"I think we should go backstage and congratulate everyone," said Miss Goodley. Grimwood, who had thought that the interval might have supplied him enough time to seek out a boiled egg, agreed reluctantly. He suspected that tensions had been apparent between the actors.

He was correct. As he, Miss Goodley and her aunt sneaked round the back, they found Headley spiting venom at everyone around him like a huge over-dressed snake. Mr Greening was trying unsuccessfully to calm him down.

"It's going well, Headley! The audience..."

"What do they know! Philistines the lot of them. The shade of the Bard must be weeping 'neath a willow in heaven. The amazing vanishing butler becomes the amazing toppling butler! And what on earth is that boy in the wellingtons doing? Where's pest control when you need them? Where is the little brat now? I'm going to hang him upside down from the woodbine on the flowery bank and stop him..."

"What ho!" said Grimwood. "Very good. We're enjoying ourselves."

Headley turned to look at the intruder with fire in his eyes. His mouth moved a great deal but no words came out.

"Very nice, Headley," said Miss Goodley. "By the way, before you hunt down and destroy Jimbo, I'd like you to meet my aunt."

Headley found voice. "Your aunt? Your aunt? Why would I want to meet your blasted aunt? Why would I want to meet anybody's blasted aunt? The only person I want to meet at the moment is the man who can rid me of toppling butlers and rogue fairies in wellingtons and..."

His demeanour changed utterly. He was looking at Miss Goodley's aunt as though at a vision from heaven. His eyebrows raised, his teeth stopped grinding and a soft, friendly light appeared in his eyes.

"Dame Judi," he said, as gentle as any sucking dove.

"Hello, Headley," said Dame Judi. "I think you're doing awfully well."

"You do?" Headley started purring with pleasure. "Well, of course, we old professionals know that whatever obstacles present themselves, the show must go on."

"Well, I think Molesbury is doing a marvellous job, and Jimbo has been the star of the show. Apart from you of course. I'd forgotten what a fine actor you are. You must give me your phone number after the show. I know a few shows in the West End that would benefit immeasurably from your presence."

Headley nearly melted. He made a strange noise that Grimwood was unable to think of a word to describe. Later, when going over the evening's events in his head, he decided it was the kind of noise a tiger might make if you tickled its tummy.

Molesbury appeared. Everyone turned to face him, and there was a general mutter of congratulation, even from the newly tamed Headley.

"Bravo, Molesbury," said Dame Judi. "Are you alright to go on, or would you like me to take over?"

"I'm afraid my age is catching up with me, Madam. I would be delighted if my understudy were to take over. It might also be easier on the fairies, who are having to do a lot of unnecessary lifting. I have no wish to be the cause of back trouble for them in later life."

"Of course. I'll need to borrow your wig."

"It slips slightly, Madam. My advice is to avoid stooping."

"I shall try. Mr. Greening, could you make an announcement? Could you tell them that I'm going to be Titania in the second half?"

Mr. Greening didn't change colour, but if he had possessed the capacity to glow like polished gold he would have done.

"This is the proudest moment of my life," he said. "Thank you, Dame Judi!" he added, punched the air, then hurried back toward the stage.

"Where's Jimbo?" said Grimwood, who had been silent and largely bemused during the exchanges. He was trying to work out why Miss Goodley's aunt had suddenly transformed into someone called Dame Judi. He knew he had heard the name before, but he couldn't think where.

"Never mind where Jimbo is," said Miss Goodley. "Second half starts soon. We'd better get out there and hear Mr. Greening's announcement. "Good luck, Aunt Judi!" she added, and left the actors to prepare.

Chapter 20

Halana looked deep into Ulf's eyes and held his hand with both of hers.

"I am so unlucky to be missing the show," said Ulf. "Thank you so much for coming and looking after me. However, I think you missing the show too is a very bad thing. I could look after myself for an hour or so, I think. There is no chance even for somebody as unlucky as me that any twitcher could fall on me here, in bed."

"I could not be leaving you by yourself, while I am having the good times with the Shakespeare. I am thinking that you would be having the loneliness, for sure." Halana looked around. "Weren't you supposed to be having the big silly dog being in your room as company?"

"I was. It was doing some of the yelping and howling because it was so miserable, and I knew how it felt, so I let it go. I told it not to leave the house though. I don't think it can get out if the front door is closed."

"Is okay and alright, Ulf. I am closed the door very much behind me, I can always remember."

*

Evil Eric stopped at his door, closed his eyes for a few moments, took some deep breaths, and spoke inwardly to himself.

"Courage, Eric. Just chop the tree down, then get out of this madhouse. Then Emma will give you the money and all will be well. Your foot feels better. There's no need to stay a second longer than you need too. The danger boy is at the play. No-one can stop you. Nothing to worry about. Just do it, and go. The boy can't be in two places at once. The women who speak strangely are at the lake too." He felt a strange pang in his heart as he thought of the woman who spoke strangely and had brought him tea and told him she liked him.

Still, despite the pep talk, he hesitated. He heard a large cheer at the lake, which subsided, leaving only his heartbeat to fill the gap. At last, he opened the door, and glanced fearfully along the corridor.

There was no-one there.

He sidled down to the stairs and tiptoed down. Still no-one interrupted him. The front door was closed, worst luck. He opened it, every creak sounding like an invitation for the devil boy to appear, brandishing an axe. His eyes widened.

The boy could not have the axe because he, Evil Eric, was clutching it in his own sweaty hands. He needed it to chop the tree down. He could defend himself if necessary. He clutched the handle of the weapon tightly to reassure himself.

The night was warm and gently moonlit. He left the door open, not wanting it to creak more than was necessary. The tree was about forty yards away. He made his way slowly towards it, all the time looking nervously around him and jumping at shadows.

He climbed the small fence that surrounded the tree, and went across to it. For some time he stood rubbing his hand against the trunk.

Why did he have to cut it down? It was just a tree. Quite a nice one, too. It suited its position well. He had enjoyed looking at it from his window. Could it really upset someone quite nasty, cutting down a tree? He supposed it could. He was feeling upset quite nasty having to do it himself. He looked upwards, and heard the leaves rustling gently in the night's breeze. It was as though the tree was trying to tell him something – perhaps a dark secret.

Come on Eric, he told himself. You're supposed to be evil.

The fence was close enough to the tree to make swinging the axe difficult.

He had an idea. His third one of the week! He felt cheered by his own hidden powers of thought, which had really come to the fore in recent times.

He climbed onto the second rung of the fence. From there, when he swung the axe, the backswing was above the fence. It gave him a lot more room to manoeuvre.

*

Bluebell was revelling in the freedom that had suddenly been allowed her. Not only had she been freed from the confines of Ulf's room, but some kind soul had left the front door of the house open and unattended. After a good sniff around the perimeter of the building, during which she came across the twin excitements of a discarded banana skin and a dead mouse, she decided to move into more open country. She had seen a squirrel earlier in the day near the tree with the fence around it, and she was keen to see if it was still around. It was now dark, of course, and her eyesight wasn't what it had been in her puppyish days, but nonetheless she thought it worth a try.

As she advanced toward the tree of squirrels, as she had mentally christened it, she had the biggest shock she had experienced in the whole of her doggy life. There, on the fence that surrounded the tree, was the fattest squirrel she had ever seen. A great, fat, slow moving squirrel, waving what looked like a giant twig about his head, and repeatedly hitting the tree with it. Why it was doing such a thing Bluebell could not imagine, but she had long ago decided that the ways of squirrels were strange and mysterious.

She stopped and sniffed the air. The wind was coming from the other direction, so that the squirrel would not smell her. To be honest, it was such a fatty she doubted if, even if it tried its utmost, it would be able to get up the tree fast enough to prevent her playing with it.

She advanced slowly and carefully, her wagging tail betraying her growing excitement. Her plan was to give the creature a cheerful nip on the backside, just enough to let it know that there was a dog around who wanted to play chase-squirrel.

When she was a few feet away, this excitement became too much for her, and she made a clumsy surge toward the corpulent rodent and sank her teeth into the skin of its rear end. To her shock and amazement, the skin came off in her mouth, and tasted like the cloth rag she had played with as a puppy. What was more, the fat squirrel yelped, and said lots of words that sounded like human words, including some she had never heard before. She rocked back on her hind legs, surprised, the cloth still in her mouth, and gazed in wonder and awe at the now clearly human form that stood in front of her, gesticulating wildly.

Evil Eric had turned to look at the mystery animal that had assaulted him. What he saw chilled his bones to the marrow and made the hairs on the back of his neck stand up like children singing hymns in school assembly.

It was a dog, but no ordinary dog.

It had horns. Small horns that looked red and shiny in the darkness, and on its back it wore a scarlet cloak that glittered and spangled under the night sky. It was clearly supernatural. This, he decided, was a dog from the dark and macabre underworld, sent no doubt by the boy, who had power over a host of minions, ghoulies, ghosts, foul beasts and other chaps that bit a man's bottom in the night.

He attempted to wave the axe in the beast's direction, but overbalanced, and fell off the fence, dropping the axe in the process. With a cry of terror he clambered to his feet, and set off towards the house. His heart and brain racing, he changed his mind, and decided to set off towards the lake, where surely the apparition would disappear under the eyes of the gathered masses.

Bluebell yelped miserably. She didn't like squirrels, but the one thing she did love was people. She couldn't get enough of them. Whether they were patting her on the head, stroking her back, giving her doggy biscuits or throwing her a stick to chase, they were undoubtedly her favourite of the lower life forms. Hence it made her sick to the stomach knowing she had clearly upset this one, and no wonder, since she had mistaken it for a fat squirrel and bitten it in a very sensitive area. The best thing to do she thought was to chase after him and give him a good lick on the face by way of an apology.

Eric stumbled ever onward, ignoring the pain in his ankle, with the vile brute giving him no peace. Not content with having ripped the rear out of his trousers, it now seemed to be trying to make a meal of his face. His terror gave him added energy and speed, and before too long he seemed to be leaving the monster a few yards behind. Taking advantage of this he picked up a thorny branch that was lying in his path and waved it in the dog's face. His efforts only seemed to provoke the beast into more frenzied face-devouring behaviour. Before long he saw lights and heard voices, and decided to take the shortest possible route into this centre of activity and live with the consequences. For some reason he heard the words 'Proceed, Moon' very loudly and clearly. He burst forth onto the stage, a hole in his trousers, a huge thorny branch in his hand and the dog at his heels.

"All I have to say," said Starveling at that point. "Is to tell you that the lantern is the moon, the thorn bush my thorn bush, and this dog my dog. He looked around at the new arrivals. "And I have brought a spare of each, just in case," he added.

The crowd roared their approval. Eric, realising the embarrassment of his position, gave a gasp, threw the thorny branch in the air, and dived off the stage like a fat squirrel jumping off a tree. Jimbo, using the unexpected distraction as an opportunity to free himself from Headley's grasp, leapt back onto the stage.

"Out dim Spot!" he yelled to no-one in particular, though Bluebell looked round, possibly thinking she had heard the name of a friend of hers.

"Bluebell!" shouted Miss Goodley, and her dog, delighted to recognise a familiar face in the crowd lost interest in her short-lived stage career and sauntered into the audience to see her mistress.

"Is it Bluebell or Spot?" shouted someone in the front row, to much laughter.

"Why, all these should be in the lantern, for all these are in the moon. But silence. Here comes Thisbe!" said Demetrius, with more than a hint of panic in his voice, and the play resumed its wayward course, though with an extra fairy sprucing up the action.

In the remaining minutes of the scene Jimbo was in his element. Perhaps wisely, he decided not to make any more verbal interjections, but his mere presence on stage added an aura of unpredictability to the proceedings that was fully in keeping with the spirit of the thing. As the rustics left the stage however, Bottom's burly hand grabbed Jimbo and led him back to the darkness behind, allowing Puck to come on and give his final summing up.

When the play was finally over the applause was rapturous from all quarters. Everyone was cheered to the rafters - or at least they would have been if the play hadn't been performed outside - and the air was filled with a sense of happiness and joy. All present realised they had just witnessed something very special indeed. The actors appeared one by one to take their share of the audience's thanks and enthusiasm. Headley, Molesbury, and Dame Judi got the second biggest cheers, but the huge roar that went up for Jimbo would have drowned out a reedbed full of bitterns.

"Jimbo was fantastic! And my Auntie was rather good too, wasn't she, Grimwood?" said Miss Goodley above the din, bursting with pride.

"Yes she was," replied Grimwood. "Absolutely splendid. She could do it professionally, in my opinion. However, I must admit I preferred Molesbury in the role."

Miss Goodley laughed. Grimwood was pleased to see her do so, even though he had been completely serious in his stated viewpoint. He didn't mind being laughed at occasionally. As long as he was making other people happy, that was the important thing. The obvious enjoyment and happiness of the people around him felt rather good, and he found himself smiling a rather silly smile.

Chapter 21

The silly smile lasted until the following morning. Halana and Ulf were the first to appear for breakfast. They held each other's hands tightly and gazed into each other's eyes in a soppy fashion.

"Good of the morning, Mr Grimwood, as the Irish would no doubt be absolutely saying very much," said Halana, who liked to think of herself as being knowledgeable and skilled in the languages of the world. "I having the good news. Myself and Ulf are to be in a wedding together."

"Yes," said Ulf. "I am the luckiest man in the world."

"Congratulations," said Grimwood. "I am very pleased to hear it."

"But I am very having sadness too, because it is the day today that we are going all back to the Netherlands, and we will be leaving each other for sure, But we are having the good times in England and I am meeting my husband to-be."

"Your husband Toby?" said Grimwood, confused. "Oh, sorry. Yes. See what you mean, now. Ulf, yes."

"Yes. I will be missing Jimbo and Moley and you mostly." She unlocked herself from her future husband and hugged Grimwood, which he rather enjoyed.

Another Halana entered, with Evil Eric on her arm.

"Good morning, Grimwood. I am having the very good news. This man here is... he is being too shy to tell you, so I will tell you very much myself. He is not being called Derek, he is being called the Eric, and he is going to be coming back to the Netherlands with me and doing the edges of the lawns and other tasks with the garden."

Grimwood lifted a sausage into the air in order to place it in his mouth, but stopped just before he did so, as a question had occurred to him.

"Why did he tell us his name was Derek? Did he forget his name?"

Eric suddenly found courage. "I'm going to confess," he said. "Everything. I was known as Evil Eric, and the lawman called Emma came to see me, and I was here to upset you quite nasty, but I didn't 'cos of the devil dog making me drop my axe, and chasing me on to the stage with no backside to my trousers and showing things I shouldn't to everyone. I upset myself quite nasty, so much so that I'm going to start a new life and start making people happy with nice lawns, and hopefully keep away from small boys and stop dropping out of windows and such." He looked at Ulf. "Sorry mate," he said, remembering how the Norwegian gentleman had broken his fall on a couple of occasions.

"It is okay. It could have happened to everyone. It was just a concatenation of circumstances, I suppose, yes?"

"I can't answer that question," said Eric.

"Aaah, I think he is going shy again," said Halana. "We must be going now and walking around the garden, and looking at the edges to the lawns. Goodbye Grimwood, and thanking you." She hugged Grimwood, which he rather enjoyed.

"Yes," he said. "For sure," he added.

They tootled off into the bright morning.

The final Halana appeared.

"Good morning to all," she said. "We are returning for to go to the Netherlands, I am not wanting to go but I must."

"Sort out the stamp situation, eh? Give them a bit of vim."

"I am not always understanding of what you are saying," said Halana, "but you are very nice. I hug you now." She did. Grimwood rather enjoyed it. "I am going back because I am having my husband missing me so much, and we have a shop which is doing the great things and selling so many stock."

"Business booming, eh?" said Grimwood. He nearly added 'like a bittern' but thought better of it.

"Yes, it is booming like a bittern," said Halana. "I must go and be doing some packing. Goodbye, Grimmychops, and thanking you!"

Jimbo ran into the room as Halana left and grabbed three sausages, with which he proceeded to juggle.

"Look everyone! I can juggle three sausages. Whoops, I dropped one. Ow," he added, as another dropped onto his head, though Grimwood doubted that the pain it caused him could have been that severe, most sausages in his experience having little weight and no sharp corners. "I've still got one though," Jimbo went on, having made a speedy recovery. "Can't stop. Got to eat my sausage and go!" He ran off, making his usual aeroplane noise.

Miss Goodley appeared from the kitchen and sat down, holding a cup of tea. A few days ago, Grimwood would have looked askance at his cook wandering in from her place of work and taking liquid refreshment with him, but now it seemed perfectly natural.

"Morning, Grimwood," she said brightly. "What a night, eh? I'm still buzzing."

"Yes, rather. Enjoyed myself. It was nice to see Mr. Greening back to his usual hue by the end of the night. His tendency to change colour according to his surroundings was alarming me. I thought only those lizard things could do that. Iguanas, are they? No, chameleons. That's it."

Miss Goodley laughed. "The only downside of the evening was that someone tried to chop your tree down, by the looks of it. The one in the garden."

"There are many in the garden, and none in the house. Which one?"

"Of course, how silly of me. The one with the fence around it. There's an axe there that someone has obviously dropped."

The remaining Halana made a strange noise with her teeth. Everyone turned to look at her. It was obvious she knew something of the matter.

"Between you and me and the breakfast items," she confided, "Halana was telling me this morning that Eric was being have been paid by a man to be chopping the tree down to upset Grimwood. But he didn't not doing it because the dog was grabbing him, and he has decided not to be bad but good now, and is sorry."

Grimwood wondered whom he could possibly have upset, since he hadn't left the house for nearly a quarter of a century. A local travel agent, perhaps, or someone who made walking boots.

"The tree is okay, though," said Miss Goodley. "There are a couple of marks in it but I'm sure it will live. I know it means a lot to you, Grimwood."

"If you are not minding that I am asking," Halana said carefully, "why is the tree being so much of importance?"

Grimwood glanced to one side, as though looking for a way to avoid the question. However, his mouth answered it for him anyway.

"Sort of a memorial. Lost my wife and little boy, a long time ago. Planted a tree." He stopped talking, and concentrated on a sausage that seemed unusually crescent-shaped. There was a few moments' silence, during which Molesbury arrived.

"Ah, Molesbury! Top of the morning," said Grimwood, pleased to have a chance to change the subject. "There's a sausage here which simply refuses to take the straightest route from A to B. You really must see it."

Molesbury looked and nodded gravely, obviously impressed. "A most unusual sausage, sir. Do you plan to eat it, or shall I place it somewhere for safekeeping?"

"The latter I think, Molesbury. We may never see its like again in our lifetime."

"Certainly, sir. I shall phone the butchers in the village and have them send out a replacement."

He took a mobile phone out of his pocket and began dialling. For a moment Grimwood looked at him in a bewildered sort of way. Then something occurred to him.

"Molesbury!" he said. "You have one of those little phones!"

"Yes, sir."

"So you could have phoned my brother at any time without going to the village!"

"Yes, sir."

"Then why didn't you?"

"It would have been pointless, sir. Jimbo is not your great-nephew. He is Miss Goodley's son, sir."

For a moment Grimwood thought his butler had suddenly grown a foot in height, but then he realised that he himself had rocked back, creating the illusion of a rapidly growing butler.

"But... but... Molesbury!"

"Yes, sir. Myself and Claire are old friends. I thought she would make a very good cook, and indeed companion, for you in your later years. She could live in the house permanently, sir, with Jimbo. I feel the house would benefit immeasurably from an injection of young blood, sir. It is a very large house and it has been rather too empty and rather too quiet over the many years we have spent alone together. I do not feel it did you any good, sir. You may have noticed a slight deterioration in your cognitive skills, sir, doubtless due to lack of stimulation. You did say you were having, fun, sir, with Jimbo in the house? I'm sure I heard you say so. Shall I finalise the arrangement, sir?"

Grimwood, unable to rock back any further without his chair capsizing, rocked forward again. Molesbury shrunk back to his usual height.

"I am leaving for the packing, now. Come on, Ulf!" Halana grabbed her fiancé's hand and left the room. Miss Goodley looked at Molesbury and then took her tea back to the safety of the kitchen, leaving the two men alone. For a while, nobody spoke. Eventually Grimwood broke the silence.

"You've not been honest with me, Molesbury."

"No, sir."

"You have not lied, but you have misled me."

"Yes, sir."

"It is not what I expect of an old butler, and, dare I say, it, friend."

"No, sir. Thank you, sir."

"But I suppose you acted with my best interests at heart."

"I always do, sir," said Molesbury. "I am hopeful that Jimbo may, one day, be your stepson, sir."

Grimwood nodded thoughtfully.

"That may well happen, Moley, if Miss Goodley is agreeable."

"I'm sure she would be delighted, sir."

Grimwood looked up at the hole in the ceiling, and thought back to the first evening Jimbo had spent at Dunnydark.

"You know, Moley, when the doorbell rang and the boy arrived, I thought the sound was the sound of angels singing."

"Indeed, sir?"

"Yes." He paused. "I think I was right. I think that is exactly what it was." He smiled gently at his old butler, who smiled respectfully back. "I think Dunnydark needs a Jimbo. I think perhaps I need one too."

"Yes, sir. I shall finalise the arrangements. Do you still want me to call the butcher's shop about the sausage?"

"No, Moley, my dear old friend. You can eat it. This calls for a celebration!"

The End

About the Author

Stephen Meek was born in Cleethorpes in 1966. He graduated in Zoology from Sheffield University in 1988. He has worked in the offices of the Automobile Association, as a double glazing salesman and in the fruit and veg section of a supermarket on the outskirts of London. He suffered from M.E. and was housebound for 5 years between 1995 and the year 2000. Now largely recovered he lives in the middle of nowhere with his wife Ruth, a lawyer, and a round orange cat called Buster. His interests include wildlife-watching, Grimsby Town Football Club, and boring everyone to death by talking about classical music in too much detail. He spends most of his time staring out of the window and taking Buster to the vets. Occasionally he writes a book and has written a volume of poetry, a fantasy novel for children and two adult novels. He is very tall but also quite fat, which makes finding trousers that fit very difficult. His ambition is to be crowned King of England.

About the Cover Artist

Sally is an illustrator and can't think of anything else that she would rather be. She spends most of her time drawing as there isn't anything else that she is good at. She lives in Lincolnshire and likes cats and drinking lots of tea. If you want to contact her regarding illustration work, or just want to chat about cats and/or tea drinking, please do so at sallytownsend@live.co.uk. You can also find a collection of her work at www.sallytownsend.co.uk

Sally graduated in 2011 with a B.A. (Hons) Illustration, School of Art and Design, University of Lincoln, U.K.

Hawkwood Books

Since 2006, Hawkwood has been publishing a variety of original, quality fiction for a wide range of ages. Our titles have received magical reviews from demanding young readers as well as informed adults.

For similar ages, you might like:

> The Fantastic Galactic Construction Kit
>
> The Fantastic Prismatic Construction Kit
>
> The Fantastic Chromatic Construction Kit (2013)
>
> The Secret
>
> Star Games
>
> The Last Garden
>
> Dinosaur Boy

For younger readers:

> Piccadilly Mitzie
>
> Byte The Computer Mite

For teenage readers, try:

> Train Ghost
>
> Miracle Girl
>
> Cool World

Full detail at: www.hawkwoodbooks.co.uk